Melissa Senate has written many novels for Harlequin and other publishers, including her debut, *See Jane Date*, which was made into a TV movie. She also wrote seven books for Harlequin's Special Edition line under the pen name Meg Maxwell. Her novels have been published in over twenty-five countries. Melissa lives on the coast of Maine with her teenage son; their rescue shepherd mix, Flash; and a lap cat named Cleo. For more information, please visit her website, melissasenate.com.

Books by Melissa Senate

Harlequin Special Edition

The Wyoming Multiples

The Baby Switch!
Detective Barelli's Legendary Triplets
Wyoming Christmas Surprise
To Keep Her Baby
A Promise for the Twins

Furever Yours

A New Leash on Love

Hurley's Homestyle Kitchen (as Meg Maxwell)

A Cowboy in the Kitchen
The Detective's 8 lb, 10 oz Surprise
The Cowboy's Big Family Tree
The Cook's Secret Ingredient
Charm School for Cowboys
Santa's Seven-Day Baby Tutorial

For my wonderful aunt and uncle,
Rick and Arlene D'Alli, who came to visit me way up
in Maine just as I was finishing writing this novel.
XOXO

Prologue

Was that a baby crying?

Nah.

Noah Dawson turned over in bed and tried to go back to sleep, but he heard the sound again. A crying baby. Impossible on this isolated ranch in the Wyoming wilderness, but unmistakable. Yesterday, Noah had gone to Bear Ridge Groceries to stock up for the impending rainstorm that threatened flash flooding, and a woman in front of him on the long checkout line had had a baby in her shopping cart, wailing just like he was hearing now. A round of peekaboo had helped quiet the screecher. But, man, did he know a crying baby when he heard one.

Still, right now? He glanced at his phone on the bedside table—at 1:52 a.m.? He had to be hearing things. Dreaming. Imagining it.

"Waaaah!"

Noah sat up. The crying was getting louder—and coming through the window on the early April breeze.

Did he have a middle-of-the-night visitor and he'd missed the doorbell ringing or something? Did he even know anyone with a baby?

"Waaah-waaah!"

Noah bolted out of bed. That *was* a baby crying. And it was coming from just outside the window of his cabin, below which was the front porch. He grabbed his jeans from where he'd slung them over his desk chair, pulled them on and hurried downstairs.

The crying got louder. He pulled the front door open.

Then he looked down—and gasped.

A baby—a girl, guessing from the pink blanket covering most of her in an infant car seat, a white cotton cap on her head—was crying up a storm. A small black tote bag was beside the carrier.

What the hell? Who would leave a baby here? He glanced around for a car, for someone, anyone, but all he saw were the distant evergreens in the moon-light. The ranch was silent otherwise.

"Hello?" he called out, looking in every direction. No one. "Hello?" he shouted.

No response. No person. Nothing but the breeze through the trees.

How long has she been out here? he wondered as he snatched up the carrier and bag and brought them inside, his heart starting to pound, his brain trying to make some sort of sense of this. A baby. Left on his porch at two in the morning.

He set the carrier on the big wood coffee table in the living room. He carefully moved aside the blanket.

Whoa. Noah didn't know much about babies, but this tiny creature had to be a newborn. He wouldn't be surprised if the baby had been born today. That's how small she was. Her pink footie pajamas were way too big for her little body.

Call the police. Call an ambulance. Call social services. So many thoughts ran through his head at once that he had to just stop, stand still and breathe.

He glanced out the window, the rain starting. Just drizzling now, but within ten to fifteen minutes the skies would open up. That was a problem. The ranch was forty minutes from town down some winding rural roads, and the storm was forecasted to quickly create flood conditions, which would come before anyone could safely reach the place. Doc Bakerton, who ran the clinic in Bear Ridge, had emergency hours, and his home was only a ten-minute drive from here. Noah could get the baby over to Bakerton's faster and safer than an ambulance or the sheriff could get here, and he knew these country roads and where the river would rise the worst. He could get back.

Decision made: he'd take her over to Doc Bakerton's place.

But right now, the baby was crying her head off. Should he comfort her for a few seconds? Noah had no idea what the hell to do. She let out another wail, and he shifted the blanket aside, not surprised she wasn't even buckled in.

Hand under the neck, he told himself, lifting her out as carefully as he could. He held her alongside his arm, bracketed by his chest, not sure he was doing this right.

He touched a finger to her little cheek. She wasn't cold or hot, and her color seemed okay.

A hot burst of anger swelled in his gut over whoever had left a newborn to the elements in the middle of the night. What if he hadn't heard her crying at all? What if she'd been out there all night? In the middle of the Wyoming wilderness, a rainstorm about to pour down. Granted, the large front porch of his foreman's cabin was covered on three sides as a point of refuge for future guests of the ranch to wait out any bad weather, but still.

He swayed his arms a bit, and the crying stopped. When the baby's strangely colored eyes—a grayish blueish—closed, his anger dissipated some. The little face looked content, relaxed, the tiny chest rising and falling, rising and falling, the impossibly tiny bow lips giving a quirk.

Whose are you? he wondered. Why would anyone leave you *here*? The Dawson Family Guest Ranch wasn't due to open for seven more weeks, on Memorial Day weekend, so the guest cabins were empty. And none of the small staff he'd hired lived on the property.

He glanced at the carrier and tote bag on the coffee table. Maybe there was a note. Or a birth certificate. Something.

He couldn't reach the bag easily without putting the baby down, and he thought he should hold her a bit—why, exactly, he wasn't entirely sure. To keep her warm? To comfort her? Make her feel connected to someone and something? His gaze caught on something small and white poking up from underneath the blanket in the car seat. He shoved the blanket aside.

So there was a note. Half a page. Scrawled, crudely, in black pen.

She's your baby, Noah Dawson. Your respon-sibility. You won't hear from me again.

Every cell in his body froze.
What?
My baby? he thought, the idea not penetrating.
Forget the police. Or social services. Until he could think, figure out who the mother was.
His baby? Seriously?
He grabbed the tote bag and rooted around inside it for a birth certificate or envelope or any kind of paperwork. Nothing but a baby bottle, a small container of formula and two tiny diapers.
The infant's eyes opened just then, then drooped, opened, drooped, then closed again. There *was* something familiar about the little face, something in the expression, the eyes, that he couldn't pin down. He *knew* that face. The baby's mother, a woman he probably was with one night… Or maybe the little girl looked a bit like him?
Just get her to the doc, he told himself. *Now.*
He very gently laid her back down in the carrier, one little fist moving, the lips quirking again. He

buckled the five-point harness and settled the blanket around her.

From the looks of her, all scrawny and tiny, tinier than your average baby, he was pretty sure she couldn't be more than a few hours old. So her mother didn't want to keep her and dropped her off right after giving birth? That hardly made sense. Mothers who'd just delivered a baby didn't jump in cars and drop off their babies in the middle of the night. Unless they were desperate, maybe.

All he knew was that someone had left a baby on his doorstep. No knock, no explanation. No concern for the infant's well-being.

No idea who that person could possibly be.

His baby? His brain wasn't fully firing right now from the shock, but as he lifted the carrier he managed to think back nine months. It was the second week of April now. Who had he been involved with last July?

There were a few possibilities. One of whom he'd seen in passing just last week as he'd parked in front of the coffee shop in town. She certainly hadn't been nine months pregnant.

Two or three others back then, one-night stands when his life had still been about drinking too much at bars and trying to forget his troubles with women whose last names he didn't know.

He wasn't proud of that time in his life.

He'd been a hot mess. Two years ago, the small ranch he'd managed to buy had gone under—like father, like son, he supposed. The woman he'd loved his entire life had told him she'd had enough and was moving on, unless he changed most things about himself. He hadn't known how, and she'd gotten tired of trying to help when all her advice fell on deaf ears. And so he'd driven her away and she'd married the biggest jerk he'd ever known. The downward spiral had continued.

And then five months ago he'd inherited the Dawson Family Guest Ranch with his five siblings, most of whom wanted nothing to do with the place. Suddenly, the man on the edge of the cliff had inched back to solid ground. Purpose. Determination. Heritage.

Before his father passed, before Noah had come back home to the formerly dilapidated guest ranch he'd grown up on, he'd had no idea heritage meant anything to him. But it clearly did. Because here he was. Not that he had anywhere else to go, but still. He wanted to be here.

And if this baby was his, she belonged here too. With him on the Dawson ranch. Until he figured out whose she was—aside from his—he'd keep his siblings out of it. Maybe he'd call his sister, Daisy, in Cheyenne. Maybe she'd come visit for a few days and help him out.

The tiny eyes opened, and her face scrunched.

"I'm taking you to the doc, little buddy."

It struck him that little girls probably weren't called "little buddy" the way boys were. He recalled how Sara—the one he'd driven away—hated that her father had called her princess. *I'm no princess*, she'd say. *Furthest thing from it.*

"You're no princess either," he told the infant. "You certainly did not get the royal treatment on your first day on earth."

Carrier in hand, he headed toward the door, setting it on the floor to put on his leather jacket. Then he picked her back up and headed out to the truck.

"I'm not gonna let anything happen to you," he said, latching the carrier rear-facing on the back seat, like the little diagram on the side of the carrier wisely showed. "You can count on that."

Chapter One

"I, Willem Michael Perry, in sound mind and body, hereby leave my second-rate wife, Sara Mayhew Perry, absolutely nothing."

Sara sat in her late husband's attorney's office, not surprised by anything in the will. The insults. The disinheritance. She wanted to run out of here, put this—including her marriage to Willem—behind her, and go home with her seven-week-old son. If she even had a home anymore.

The lawyer, Holton Parrington, who'd grimaced

through every word of the will as he'd read it aloud, put the document down on his desk and took off his glasses. "Sorry about all this, Sara," he said, shaking his head. "Willem wasn't exactly the nicest person, was he?"

Understatement of the year. Decade, maybe. But you make a deal with the devil… "No, he wasn't."

Her husband had died in a car accident five days ago. He hadn't been a good person, but Sara hadn't married him for his personality. She knew she wasn't perfect, but doing what needed to be done had always come naturally to her, and she'd hoped she could help Willem change, that she would rub off on him, that impending fatherhood would mean something to him, but he'd actually gotten meaner, more spiteful, more controlling.

She glanced at the stroller to her left; baby Chance slept peacefully. She kept her gaze on him for a moment longer; her son was all that truly mattered. Nothing else.

"Willem also left a letter to you and instructions that I read it aloud in the event of his death," Holton continued. "It's sealed, and I have no idea what's inside. Ready?"

Sara sighed inwardly. "For more bashing? No. But I guess this will be the end of it."

The lawyer nodded. He put his glasses back on,

then slit open the envelope and pulled out one sheet of paper, written in Willem Perry's unmistakable, perfect handwriting.

"'Sara, if you're reading this, I'm dead,'" the lawyer read, pausing as if bracing himself. He cleared his throat and continued. "'I don't know what got me in the end, but I hope it was quick and painless and that I lived till at least ninety-three like my father.'"

Willem hadn't made it to his twenty-ninth birthday. He'd been reckless with the brand-new Porsche, a gift to himself for becoming a father, and had been going more than ninety around the rain-slick curve on the winding service road into town.

"'I debated about putting what I'm about to say on paper,'" the lawyer continued reading, "'but decided I couldn't—make that shouldn't—take it to the grave with me. Oh yes, I want you to know. You deserve to know. Brace yourself, darlin'.'"

She was already doing that. Who knew what Willem was capable of? She did, actually. She wished she'd known the extent of his cruelty before she'd agreed to marry him. She'd known he was a snob, but he'd been so kind to her before their wedding, and she'd had such faith she'd turn him around. Back then, she'd thought his worst trait was talking down to waitstaff in the nice restaurants he'd taken her to.

She'd never take anything at face value again. That was for damned sure.

She sucked in a deep breath. *Whatever it is, whatever his last laugh is, I can take it*, she told herself. *I'm stronger than I know. Just keep chanting that and maybe it'll be true.*

The attorney glanced at her, and she nodded.

"'Our son's twin sister didn't die during childbirth,'" the lawyer read on a gasp, his eyes widening.

Sara gasped too. *What?* They stared at each other, his face as pale as hers must be.

The lawyer sucked in a breath and continued reading. "'The female twin was frail, much smaller than the male. But very much alive. Thank God I'd insisted on a home birth with a midwife, or I'd never have been able to do what I did.'"

She grabbed the sides of the chair. Her mind went blank, the air whooshing out of her, blackness threatening. *What did you do, Willem? What the hell did you do?*

The lawyer leaned back, took off his glasses and scrubbed a hand over his face.

"Finish the letter," Sara said, hearing the panic rise in her voice.

What happened to my baby girl?

Holton nodded, his expression grim. "'I threatened the midwife and paid her off not to call for medical intervention and to back me up when I told you the female didn't survive the birth. Don't be too hard on the poor lady. She accepted the bribe for the same reason you married me. She desperately needed the money.'"

The lawyer glanced at her then, and Sara, feeling her face flame, lifted her chin.

"'I told you the baby died,'" the lawyer continued reading, "'then while you were sleeping, I drove it out to Noah Dawson's place—'"

Sara bolted up. "Noah? Noah has my daughter?"

Her head was spinning. Her daughter was alive? And with Noah Dawson?

"Let's finish the letter," Holton said. "There's only one paragraph left."

Sara nodded, tears brimming as she dropped back on the chair.

The attorney cleared his throat. "'With my male heir healthy, I had no need for a sickly-looking daughter. To be quite honest, I don't particularly *like* girls. They grow up to become conniving users, don't they? I drove the baby out to Dawson's cabin and left her on his porch with that starter kit the midwife had on hand and a note saying it was his baby and his responsibility. For all I know, the twins *are* his. Maybe you were cheating on me with him during our entire marriage. Since I don't know whether any of that is true, it means it could be. Since it could also not be, I'll leave my son the bulk of my estate in trust for when he turns twenty-one. The rest will go to the development of a golf course named in my honor. You, as you already know, get nothing. Not a cent.'" The lawyer paused and put down the letter. "That's the extent of it. It's signed 'Willem Michael Perry.'"

My daughter didn't die. She's alive.

"For the past seven weeks, Noah Dawson has had my daughter?" she whispered, the blackness threatening again.

She tried to remember back to the moment when the midwife—a gentle woman in her early sixties who'd come highly recommended—placed Chance on her chest. Tears had been brimming in the woman's eyes over what Sara had assumed was the loss of the baby girl she'd helped deliver. Sara had felt so woozy, despite Willem's insistence she take no drugs. She must have fallen asleep hard after initially nursing Chance, because she'd woken up hours later, Willem letting her know Chance was sleeping like a champ in the nursery and that the midwife had gone home and that they'd taken care of the details for the loss of the twin.

She'd been so woozy still, her head feeling like it was stuffed with cotton, and she'd been so grateful that she hadn't lost both babies that she'd made her way to the nursery and held Chance against her. Her precious son had gotten her through the terrible truth that his sister hadn't survived. Over the next few days, Willem had resumed his usual twelve-hours-per-day work schedule, so she hadn't had to deal with him controlling her in person, though he'd left detailed emails about how to hold Chance, feed him, his nap schedule, and that no one was to visit until he'd had his shots.

Her baby girl was alive. And Sara wouldn't be the least bit surprised if Willem had slipped something into her water during labor, some kind of drug to keep her off balance and to make her sleep hard afterward.

Why would he take the baby to Noah, though? Willem had hated Noah Dawson.

"Sara, I'm afraid I have to prepare you for the possibility that the female twin didn't survive Willem's actions," the lawyer said, shaking her out of her question. "Left on a doorstep in the middle of the night? The second week of April, when it was still a bit chilly? Who knows when Mr. Dawson discovered the baby? If he was even home at the time? Didn't he very recently inherit the old Dawson guest ranch? I read that they're set for a grand opening this weekend, but I can't imagine how, given how run-down the place was."

She hadn't known Dawson's was reopening. She'd heard that Noah's widowed father had died and that he'd left the dilapidated ranch to his six children. She'd thought about going to the funeral but wasn't sure she'd be welcome. She'd been showing then and didn't want to make Noah uncomfortable, so she'd stayed home. She also would have had to get around Willem about where she was going, and she hadn't had the energy for that.

When she'd woken up about three hours after giving birth, the rain had been coming down hard. Willem had left their daughter on a ranch porch in the middle of the night during a rainstorm? The Dawson ranch in Bear Ridge was over an hour away from the Perry house in Wellington.

She swallowed back a wail building up deep inside her. "I'm going to see Noah now. My daughter is alive. I feel it."

"I hope so, Sara," Holton said. "It seems clear that Willem expected this letter to be read decades from now. There are two bombshells, really. Your daughter. And the midwife's culpability. We can discuss options for how to proceed there."

She'd deal with that later. Right now, she only wanted to see her baby girl with her own eyes. Hold her. Get her *back*.

She reached for her long cardigan and put it on,

then gripped the handle of Chance's stroller. He was fast asleep.

"Sara, again, I'm very sorry," Holton said. "I hate to bring this up right now, but I do need to tell you that you'll need to vacate the house within fourteen days. You may take your personal possessions, but everything else now belongs to the estate. If there's anything you'd like to take, do it before tomorrow, when the appraisals will begin."

She nodded again. She couldn't wait to leave that house. Where she'd move, she had no idea. But she did know where she was going now.

To see Noah Dawson. And get her baby girl.

"Should we give Bolt an apple slice?" Noah asked his baby daughter, snug in the carrier strapped to his chest.

He stood at Bolt's stall in front of the small barn beside his cabin, the mare nudging his arm for her apple. "We should? I agree." He pulled the baggie of apple slices from his pocket.

Annabel didn't respond, but according to the book on your baby's first year, she wouldn't make sounds or coo for another couple of weeks.

He'd learned quite a bit about babies in the past seven weeks. He'd been right that Annabel had only been hours old when she'd been left on his porch.

Doc Bakerton had been a grouch at being woken up at 2:20 in the morning—until he'd seen why Noah had come blazing over.

Because Bakerton was getting up there in years—nearing eighty—and had long been a rural doctor, he hadn't said anything about calling the sheriff or social services. Noah had showed him the note he'd found in the carrier, and that had been good enough. "The system doesn't need another abandoned baby when the perfectly good father is standing up," the doctor had said with a firm nod. Bakerton declared the infant healthy but small, recommended two possible pediatricians to follow up with and sent Noah on his way to beat the worst of the rain.

And so a little over twenty minutes after arriving, Noah had taken the baby home, shell-shocked but focused on the immediate here and now, not even tomorrow. The doc had given Noah some samples of formula and more diapers and wipes and had made a list of the basics Noah should buy in the morning.

Some of the shock had started to wear off while he'd been at Bakerton's, mostly because he'd realized he *could* simply leave the infant with the doctor, who'd call whoever needed to be called. The sheriff. Social services. And that would be that.

But what Bakerton had said kept echoing in his head as he'd watched him move that little stethoscope around the tiny back and chest...*when the perfectly good father is standing up.*

Noah Dawson, perfectly good father? He would have burst out laughing if the situation hadn't been so incredibly lacking in humor. Thing was, after all that he'd been through, all he'd lost, after the bad day he'd had with a sick calf, Noah had appreciated the extra show of faith in himself as a human being, and Bakerton had uttered the right words at exactly the right moment. The note said the baby was his. The perfectly good—or *able*, he figured Bakerton had meant—father was here with the infant, doing exactly what he should be doing. That was two for two on the faith scale.

He'd driven slow as his late grandmother's molasses back to the ranch in the pouring rain, and once inside he'd gone straight to his laptop, holding the tiny baby along his arm as he watched a YouTube video on how to mix formula, how to hold the bottle—how to hold a newborn, for that matter. Turns out he hadn't been doing that too wrong. He'd watched each video twice. By the time he'd closed his laptop, word had come that the river had flooded and two roads into town were impassable. He'd breathed a sigh of relief at the timing; the baby was safe and had been checked out, and Noah had what he'd needed to get through the night. The universe had been looking out for Noah lately.

They'd both survived that first night. While feeding the tiny infant, he'd realized he'd have to name her, and Annabel popped into his mind and that was that. He'd refused to let himself dwell on why.

Annabel Dawson. It wasn't official anywhere, not yet, but he'd have to deal with that too—getting Annabel a birth certificate while worrying that some bureaucrat would demand he hand his baby over.

His baby.

How Noah had gotten from where he'd been the night he'd found Annabel to *his baby* rolling off his tongue with ease was anyone's guess, but it had happened, and no one was more surprised than his sister. When the roosters had announced it was officially morning, he'd called his sister, Daisy, who lived out in Cheyenne, and boy, had she been in shock. She'd driven up by early evening and helped him so much—with Annabel and the ranch—the baby making her smile when he'd catch her looking so worried so often. Daisy had been close to five months pregnant then and wouldn't say a word about who the father was. She'd seemed relieved to have a reason to move somewhere, even to the family ranch, with its tangled roots and all.

Up until the moment he'd found Annabel, he'd

spent the four months prior rebuilding the Dawson
Family Guest Ranch. That had changed him, turned
him around, made him a better person and had to
have *something* to do with how immediately responsible he'd felt for the baby left on his porch—his
baby. Add that to a tiny finger clutching his pinkie
while feeding her. Being up all hours of the night
checking on her—sometimes just to make sure she
was still breathing. Googling "lullabies newborns
like" and then playing them, and then singing them
himself while sitting in the rocker he'd gotten from
the town swap shop. Changing diapers. Playing peekaboo. Reading the pertinent pages of *Your Baby's
First Year* and googling all the little things Annabel
did that he wasn't sure was normal. Like burping so
loud from that tiny body.

During the past seven weeks, he and Annabel had
gotten even closer with all the walking around the
vast property of the ranch, the baby against his chest
in the Snugli and cozy footie pajamas. He'd told her
all about the history of the ranch—how his grandparents had built it fifty-two years ago, how popular
it had once been with tourists and locals coming to
relax out in the country, to hike or ride on the vast
trails in the woods and open grasslands, to learn to
ride a horse, shear a sheep, spin fleece into yarn, milk
cows and goats, and make butter and yogurt and his

grandmother's award-winning ice cream, which she'd sold right in their own little shop in the main barn. Bess Dawson had always handed each of her grandchildren a little spoon and sample cup of her new flavors to make sure the ice cream passed the kid test, and every flavor always had. Noah could still taste his favorites: chocolate-chocolate chip, strawberry, Bear Ridge Mix—pistachio ice cream with peanuts. Noah had also told Annabel how his widowed father had destroyed it all within three years of inheriting the place, drinking and gambling away profits, savings, their legacy, his six kids eventually scattering across the West to get away from him.

Noah was the youngest and had been trapped there for a good bunch of those low years. Daisy, two years older, watched over him the best she could until she'd been driven away by their dad's self-destruction when she was eighteen. Noah had also left the moment he'd become a legal adult, all his pleading to his father to get his act together going in one ear...

Ten years later, the Dawson Family Guest Ranch had been a ghost ranch, rarely mentioned anymore except for someone in town to shake their head over its demise. But with the money Noah and his siblings had invested, he and a hardworking crew had gotten the place in shape—albeit on a smaller scale than the original—in just five months so they could open Memorial Day weekend. The day after tomorrow, Friday, was the grand reopening. His brothers hadn't responded to his invitation to stop by for the big day, and Noah wouldn't be surprised when none showed up.

"Let the place go," the Dawson siblings had all said to Noah one way or another at their father's funeral.

Except Noah hadn't been able to—and then his siblings had rallied around him, making a plan to invest in rebuilding because doing so meant something to him and would mean everything to their grandparents. Noah wouldn't ever let the ranch go. For many reasons. So many reasons he hadn't even told Annabel all of them yet. And he'd told her just about everything. His confidante was a seven-week-old, ten-pound, nine-ounce baby with chubby cheeks. There was a first for everything.

He heard a car coming up the drive and turned around. A silver Range Rover SUV was barreling up the dirt road toward the foreman's cabin. Did he know anyone who drove a Range Rover? The eldest Dawson sibling, Ford, maybe. But Ford had also said hell would freeze before he'd step foot on the ranch again.

Whoever it was sure was in a hell of a hurry to get to the cabin.

One hand protectively on the back of Annabel's head in the Snugli, he watched the SUV suddenly come to a dead stop halfway up the drive. The glare from the sun made it impossible to see who was behind the wheel. Why stop there?

The Range Rover suddenly started up again and inched forward, this time at two miles an hour.

When the SUV finally got within a few feet, he could see inside.

Holy hell.

Sara.

How long had it been? Almost two years. After she'd told him she was marrying Willem Perry—he could barely even think the name in his head without wanting to vomit or hit something—he'd then heard they'd moved out to Wellington, an affluent town an hour away. He hadn't seen or heard from her since. He'd been close with Sara's only living relative, her father, but Preston Mayhew had gotten very sick a few months before she'd married Willem. He'd also heard Sara had had her dad transferred from the county hospital to the state-of-the-art one in Wellington. Noah had once called about visiting hours and was told that all visitors had to be preapproved by Willem Perry. So much for that. It was better that there was no one to talk to him about Sara or what she was up to or how great her life was with that bastard Willem; Noah wouldn't have been able to bear it.

The car door opened and she stepped out, and his heart lurched. That wasn't a surprise. The sight of Sara Mayhew had always had that effect. Not just because she was so pretty with her silky light brown hair and round, pale brown eyes; his attraction to her had always been about who she was, not how good she looked. Though she did look good.

She must have heard about the Dawson Family Guest Ranch reopening this weekend and decided to check the place out for herself. After all, she'd grown up here too.

"I can't tell you how great it is to see you, Sara," he said, surprising even himself with his honesty. But it was bursting out of him. He'd missed her so much the past couple of years that he'd done regretful things to forget her, nothing working.

She shut her car door and walked toward him, her gaze on the Snugli, then moving up to his face. "You found that baby on your porch seven weeks ago? The early-morning hours of April 9?" Her voice sounded strange. Desperate and shaky.

He stared at her, his grip a bit tighter on the baby carrier. "How did you know that?"

"Because Willem—my late husband—is the one who put her there. She's mine, Noah. My daughter."

What? Noah took a step toward Sara, then a step back. "There was a note with her. It said she's mine."

Sara shook her head. "She's not yours. Willem told me she died during the home birth. But he just didn't want her because she was a girl and frail-looking when her healthy, robust twin brother—the male heir—had been born two minutes earlier."

No. That's insanity. On what planet does that sound believable? Even the worst of the worst like Willem Perry wouldn't do something like that. To his own flesh and blood? His newborn daughter?

She stepped forward, her gaze on the baby's head before looking up at him. "He left a letter for me via his lawyer detailing how he drove her here right before the rain started to come down in the middle of the night. I had no idea. I thought she didn't survive the birth." A sob escaped her, and she put her hand over her mouth.

Oh God. Unthinkable.

So unthinkable that it wasn't quite sinking in. All he could do in the moment was look at Annabel, whom he'd taken care of for the past almost two months, whom he *loved.* She was his daughter. The note had said so. She was *his* child.

"That's my baby girl, Noah," she said, taking another step, then stopping. Maybe because of the expression on his face, which had to be something like horror.

For a second he could only stare at Sara, trying to process the craziness that had just come out of her mouth.

He thought about the first moments after bringing Annabel inside the night he'd found her. There had been something familiar about the little face, something in the expression, the eyes, that he couldn't pin down. He'd figured the baby's mother was a woman he'd been with for one night...

He and Sara had made love hundreds of times during their brief time as a couple, but the last time was right before she'd dumped him two years ago. He certainly wasn't the father of her daughter.

He glanced down at what he could see of Annabel's little profile, and yup, there it was, that slight something in the turndown of the eyes, the way the mouth curved upward. It was Sara's face. No wonder he'd felt so strangely connected to Annabel from the moment he'd brought her inside the cabin—before he'd even read the note falsely declaring the baby was his.

"I want to hold her so badly," Sara said. She reached out, and Noah felt the surrender everywhere in his body—the region of his heart most pointedly. This was Sara's baby. Not his.

Hell, he might break down crying. But he lifted Annabel out of the carrier. He handed her over with a stabbing awareness that this was it—it was over. His stint at fatherhood. He was proud of what he'd accomplished with the ranch, but he was proudest of what he'd accomplished with his daughter.

Not his daughter. He'd have to take that phrasing out of his vocabulary, out of his head. She wasn't his.

As Sara clutched the baby to her chest, tears streaming down her face, he closed his eyes, not surprised by the weight of sadness crushing his chest.

He loved Annabel. *That* was a surprise. But it was true.

"Is there somewhere I can go to spend time with her?" Sara asked, her gaze moving from the baby to Noah as she gently touched her wispy light brown curls, her cheek, her arm, her little fingers. "I just can't believe this is real."

Me either. He stared at his daughter—*her* daughter—and the jab in his chest intensified.

"You can take her into the cabin," he said. "She's eaten recently and been changed, so she's all set."

Now she stared at *him*, as if shocked he knew anything about Annabel's feeding and diaper-changing schedule.

"My son, her twin brother, is in the SUV," Sara

said. "Could you take him out for me? I can't bear to let go of my daughter."

My daughter. My daughter. My daughter.

Noah's head was swimming, and his knees were wobbly. He nodded and lurched toward the Range Rover, mostly to have something to brace his fall if his legs did give out.

He pulled open the door, and there was Annabel's honest-to-goodness twin in green-and-white-striped pajamas. They looked so much alike—the wispy light brown curls. The slate-blue eyes. The nose. The expression. It was all Sara.

He took out the car seat and brought it around to where Sara stood. He lifted up the seat to Annabel's level. The baby that had been in his arms until five minutes ago. "Annabel, you're about to meet your twin brother."

Sara's mouth dropped open. "Annabel? That's what you named her?"

He nodded. It was Sara's middle name.

Tears filled her eyes, and she blinked hard.

"This is Chance," she said. "Chance, meet Noah Dawson. I've known him a long time."

A very long time. "Very nice to meet you, Chance." He gently touched a hand to the downy little head with its soft brown wisps.

"And Chance, this is Annabel, your twin sister,"

Sara added. "You're back together where you belong."

Oh hell. He was about to break down himself.

"I want to hear everything," she said, her pale brown eyes imploring. "From the moment you realized she was outside on your porch to the moment I drove up. I need to know about her life these past seven weeks. But first I just need some time alone with her. To let this sink in." She cuddled Annabel against her, her gaze going from her daughter to Noah and back again.

All these weeks that Annabel had been right here, with him, her mother had believed that her baby girl was dead. He had to stop thinking about himself and focus on that—what Sara had been through.

And how twin babies had almost been separated forever.

"I understand," he said, the sturdy weight of the car seat in his right hand making him both happy and miserable. "I'll help you inside with the twins, and you can have the place to yourself for however long you need. Text me when you're ready and I'll come fill you in."

She let out a breath. "Thank you, Noah. You can't imagine." She shook her head, her tear-streaked face his undoing as much as the situation.

He *couldn't* imagine.

They started walking to the cabin, which had once been her home when her father had been foreman. She stopped for a moment, staring up at the newly renovated two-story log house with the hunter green covered porch and flower boxes his sister had insisted on putting everywhere. Sara didn't say anything about the place, how it had changed, but she had much bigger things on her mind than the ranch.

He opened the door, then stepped aside so she could enter with Annabel. He followed her in, wanting to rip his daughter from her arms. He had to stop walking for a second; the pain in his chest was that severe, and dammit, he was worried he'd start bawling like a little kid any second.

He led her into the living room and set Chance's carrier on the floor beside the sofa. Sara dropped down on the sofa, crying, laughing, staring at the baby girl in her arms.

"Her baby bag is on the stroller by the door if you need anything," he managed to say. "Plus, there's a big basket of baby stuff on the side of the coffee table."

She couldn't take her eyes off Annabel. She nodded as if barely able to hear him.

"Take as long as you want," he said. "Text me when you're ready for me to come back and we'll talk." He jotted his cell number down and left it on the coffee table.

She nodded, not taking her eyes off her daughter.

He wanted to grab Annabel away from her and run. Or just stay here, not letting the baby girl out of his sight.

Because no matter how many times he told himself she wasn't his daughter, he couldn't make himself believe it.

He forced himself out the door, his heart staying behind.

Chapter Two

Sara couldn't stop staring at the tiny baby nestled against her chest. Couldn't stop touching her, couldn't stop telling her she loved her, that she was so sorry she hadn't been there the past seven weeks, that nothing would ever come between them again.

On the drive over to the ranch from the lawyer's office, she'd kept thinking, *Please let my daughter be alive. Please let her be there. Please, please, please.* Her prayers answered, Sara's relief, her pure joy at being reunited with her baby girl, trounced her anger—murderous rage, really, at what had been done to the infant, done to Sara. *That monster took so much from us. He's not getting a second more of any piece of me. Not my thoughts or my emotions. Nothing. He's gone.*

"We have so much to catch up on," Sara whispered, in awe of everything about Annabel. Her ten fingers and toes. Her little nose and chin. The way her chest rose and fell in her sea-foam-green-and-white pajamas with little ducklings across the front. That she was really, truly *here*.

The baby's eyes were drooping, and Sara would be happy to sit here forever with Annabel napping in her arms. She glanced down at Chance, who was already asleep in his carrier. The siblings, twins, back together. She took in a deep, satisfying breath. Seven weeks felt like so much to miss out on, but she knew as time went on, she'd be grateful it had barely been two months.

She stood up, gently rocking Annabel, and walked over to the stone fireplace that dominated one wall of the living room, photos on the mantel. She'd lived in this house from the time she was born until she was sixteen, had sat on the sofa facing that fireplace night after night with her father after her mother passed away when she was nine. Talks, homework, reading, her dad's delicious sub sandwiches as they watched a series they could enjoy together. Her entire life was up in the air right now, but being here in this cabin made her feel safe.

"I grew up here," she whispered to Annabel. "Your grandma lived here. And your grandfather loved this cabin. He was the foreman here." Now Noah was.

She froze, biting her lip as Noah's words came back to her. *There was a note with her. It said she was mine.*

All this time, Noah had thought the baby was his. She glanced around the room, taking in the pale yellow playpen with its pastel mobile atop it by the bay window. The baby swing. The big basket of baby paraphernalia by the coffee table—she could see neatly folded burp cloths, a pack of diapers, a pink pacifier on a silver tray on the coffee table. An infant stroller was by the front door with a tote bag hanging from its handles. Lots of photos on the mantel were of Annabel, a few of Noah holding her.

She gasped as it *really* sank in that Annabel had lived here these past seven weeks, that Noah had taken her in—as his daughter.

Was he relieved that the mother had come back to take her? Upset? Noah Dawson was the bachelor of bachelors. Clearly he'd gotten his act together to reopen the guest ranch, but perhaps his siblings were all involved in that. The Noah she'd known near the end of their relationship two years ago didn't wake until noon, despite having a ranch to run. Didn't take care of business. Didn't take care of their fledgling romance, the one she'd fought and kicked so hard for. Turned out Noah Dawson had been right about himself—that he'd only break her heart in more ways than one.

She always thought she knew better, didn't she.

Her future was in her arms. In the carrier beside the sofa. Her children. Hours ago she'd had only a son. Now she had twins.

Take the blessing and let that fill you, she ordered herself. Because letting herself get caught up in anger over the past—recent and not so recent—would only hold her back. She had a family to raise, money to earn, a life to start.

She took a deep breath and glanced at the other photos on the mantel, surprised to see one of her and Noah in their caps and gowns, their high school graduation. They'd both worked at the Circle D then, a prosperous ranch a half hour away. Sara had lived there as the foreman's daughter, and Noah was a hand. But a month later, when he turned eighteen, Noah had moved there too, so upset by the conversation he'd had with his dad a half hour earlier that he'd gone off alone. Sara still didn't know what had gone on during that discussion.

The other photos were of his siblings, the six of them together when Noah was sixteen. They'd still come home to celebrate his birthday, though they'd refused to have Christmas at the ranch with their dad and had flown Noah to one of their homes instead.

There was a photo of his mom, a pretty brunette with blue eyes who'd died when he was ten, something that had brought Sara and Noah even closer. They never had to talk about how awful it felt to miss your mother, to wish she were there. They just knew and could be together, quiet, skipping stones in the river, throwing bread to the ducks, climbing trees and sitting up there for hours.

She missed the Noah he'd been three-quarters of the time—even to the very end of their relationship two years ago. She missed that guy so, so much.

And she'd missed this cabin. She turned to look around. She had so many memories here, so much history. She knew every nook and cranny, which floorboards creaked on the stairs, how many steps it was down to the creek (182), how she'd sat on her bed in her room upstairs, writing *Sara Dawson* in hearts in her journal like the lovesick teenager she'd been.

"Where's my sweet baby girl?" a woman's voice called cheerily through the front screen door, followed by a set of knocks. "I need my Annabelly time."

Sara froze. Oh God. Who was this?

Noah's wife? Girlfriend?

"Noah? You here?" the feminine voice called.

Sara bit her lip. Should she go to the door? Pretend she wasn't here?

Curiosity got the better of her, since this woman might have helped Noah take care of Annabel the past seven weeks. Maybe, in fact, she'd done all the work. That was more likely.

She went to the door, and her heart soared. It was Daisy Dawson, Noah's only sister.

"Daisy!" Sara said, hearing her voice break and not caring. Her long honey-brown hair in a braid practically to her waist, a straw cowboy hat on her head, pretty, sweet Daisy had been a good friend from childhood until Willem had isolated Sara from everyone she used to care about. Daisy was also at least six months pregnant.

"Whoa—Sara?" Daisy asked with a shocked grin, pulling open the screen door and coming inside. She glanced at Annabel in Sara's arms. "This is a huge surprise. Did you come for Dawson's grand reopening?" Before Sara could even respond, Daisy added, "That rascal Noah—he didn't even tell me you two had gotten back in touch. God, Sara, it's so good to see you. You look amazing. So healthy and glowy. Is Noah here or did he have to step out to deal with something?" Daisy touched a finger to Annabel's cheek. "I'm so glad you got to meet my beautiful niece. Isn't she precious?"

My beautiful niece. Sara's knees buckled.

Sara tightened her arms around Annabel, more out of instinct than because she was worried she'd really drop to her knees.

Her every emotion must have been showing on her face, because Daisy tilted her head and looked at her. "Sara? You okay?"

"Not really," Sara said. "Not by a long shot. I'll be okay, though."

Daisy put a hand on Sara's arm, her warm blue eyes filled with concern. "How about we go talk in the kitchen? I know I could use a cup of decaf. I actually could use a big mug of real coffee. But I'm limiting myself to one cup a day, and I had that." She patted her belly.

Sara glanced at Daisy's left hand. No ring. She wondered what the story was there as she followed Daisy into the kitchen. Daisy always used to talk about wanting to be a mom one day, but she was insistent on picking the right guy so she'd never get divorced like her parents had, let alone thrice divorced like her dad. Sara had once pointed out that you could pick the right guy, as her own mother had, and leave him a brokenhearted widow at age thirty-six. You just never knew what life was going to throw at you.

As Daisy headed for the coffee maker, reaching for two mugs in the cabinet, Sara found her attention taken by the refrigerator door, all the things hung up with magnets. There was a checklist of baby-proofing essentials. A cutout newspaper ad for a local grandmother of five who did hand embroidery personalization on baby clothing and blankets and towels. The American Academy of Pediatrics' recommendations for feeding and napping schedules.

"Noah loves Annabel, doesn't he," Sara said, more a statement than a question, her voice sounding far away to her own ears as she stood in front of the fridge. "I can tell. I knew it as soon I saw him with her in the Snugli."

Daisy tilted her head. "Of course. He loves that baby girl to pieces. Did you hear the crazy story? How someone left her on his porch right before that terrible rainstorm just about two months ago? There was a note that said the baby was his. He had no reason to doubt it. He even insists Annabel looks like him, but I don't see it. Don't tell him I said that!" She laughed and pressed a button on the coffee maker.

Sara almost smiled at the thought of Noah thinking Annabel looked like him. Once upon a time, when she'd still held out hope for marrying Noah

Dawson and having a family with him, she'd always pictured little Noahs, two or three, with intense blue eyes and wavy dark hair, mischievous grins and big hearts.

"Daisy, I have a crazier story," Sara said. And told her everything. Not leaving a detail out.

Daisy was an expressive woman to start with, but the range of emotions that crossed her face was something. "Oh my God, Sara."

Sara nodded.

"Can I be really happy for you and really sad for my brother at the same time?" Daisy asked. "He must be out of his mind right now knowing you're going to take Annabel away."

Take Annabel away. Sara's stomach flipped over. She'd never really thought of coming to get her daughter as taking the baby away from someone. But now she kept seeing the look on Noah's face as he'd taken Annabel out of the carrier and handed her over.

It was anguish.

Oh, Noah, she thought. *This part of the story never would have occurred to me.*

This whole time, from the moment the lawyer had read Willem's awful letter, Sara had only focused on the fact that her daughter was alive, that Willem had taken her to Noah's cabin. She'd never stopped to think about what had happened between then and now. Sara had just wanted to find her child and reunite.

But Noah had taken her in, had been raising her as his own, as he believed she was.

And that anguish on his face? Yes, he loved the baby.

Daisy poured two mugs of coffee and then opened Noah's fridge. "Ooh, half a pecan pie. I think we're gonna need a little of that too. Maybe a lot. Am I right?"

"Probably," Sara said. "I'm not sure if I can eat a bite of anything, but since when don't I stress eat?"

Daisy nodded sagely and grabbed the pie and the container of half-and-half, and Sara brought over the mugs to the table. By the time Sara sat down and took her third sip of the coffee and her second bite of pie, an idea had started forming in her mind.

An either really good idea or a really bad one. She truly wasn't sure.

Noah barely heard what his ranch hand was saying about the hay bales, but the guy was smiling, so Noah smiled back and nodded. Two days before the grand opening was no time to have his mind elsewhere, but every cell in Noah's body was focused on his cabin. And what was going on in there.

He knew, actually. Sara was reuniting with the daughter she'd never gotten to hold. Never gotten to meet, let alone know.

And soon she'd text him that she was ready for him to come back so they could talk, so he could fill her in on the last seven weeks.

So he could say goodbye to the baby girl he'd taken care of. His daughter who wasn't.

The pain gripped his chest again, and he sucked in a breath.

"You okay, boss?" Dylan asked, adjusting his cowboy hat as he peered at Noah. "You don't look so good."

"A-okay," Noah assured him. "So everything's in order in the main barn. What about the petting zoo?"

Dylan nodded, his mop of blond bangs shifting. "We're all set. I did inventory this morning. We won't need to place orders till Tuesday. Layla's feeding the farm animals now."

Noah nodded. "Thanks," he said. He'd hired several experienced hands for the land and animals and knew he could let go for a little while to deal with what was going on with Annabel.

He walked the quarter mile to his cabin and saddled up Bolt, riding her out to the gate a half mile down the gravel drive. He stopped and patted Bolt's flanks, staring at the hunter green metal that stretched across the road, Dawson Family Guest Ranch in gold letters, the silhouettes of a cowboy and a cowgirl on horses on either side. His grandparents had made belt buckles with the logo to sell in the gift shop, and one Christmas, he'd had six personalized with the grandkids' names. Noah still had his. In fact, he kept it on his desk, always had, and the past five months the buckle had served as a talisman, a lucky charm.

And for the past seven weeks, Annabel's presence had spurred him on to go even farther with making sure every detail of the ranch's reopening was perfect. This was going to be her future.

Now she wouldn't be part of it. She wouldn't be around at all.

His phone pinged with a text, and he reluctantly took it from his pocket. The sooner Sara was ready for him to return, the sooner she'd leave. With his baby.

But it was Daisy texting him.

U ok? Where R U? Heard whole story from S in the cabin.

At the gate, he texted back. No, not OK.

She texted back, Be right there.

A few minutes later, Daisy rode up on her bike.

She jumped off, one hand on her belly, and threw her arms around him.

"Sara's going to take her away," Noah said, letting his sister comfort him for a second before pulling back. He stared out at the woods beyond the road. "Just like that."

"I'm so sorry," Daisy said. "You know I love that baby girl."

"At least Annabel will be with her mother. And Sara will be with her daughter. I should focus on that. She got her daughter back. It's a friggin' miracle."

Daisy nodded. "It is."

"And I guess Annabel as a Perry and not a Dawson will have every creature comfort, certainly more than I could ever provide." He knew the Dawson Family Guest Ranch would do well; he was already booked for the weekend and had bookings stretching all the way to fall. Not every cabin was filled for every day, but word of mouth would spread, and the ranch would be a big success. He believed it. But he'd never be able to give Annabel the life Sara could as richer-than-rich Willem Perry's widow.

"You know what's crazy, Daize?" he said. "My heart's been broken before, so I know what that feels like. This feels like that."

His sister put her hand on his arm. "Look, I don't know what happened between you and Sara two years ago. But maybe you can stay in touch, visit Annabel."

He could just see it now. "Uncle" Noah coming to visit every couple of months, bringing a stuffed animal. How could he become Uncle Noah when that baby had changed his entire life and world? She'd turned him into a father, something he wouldn't have seen coming in a million years. And dammit, he'd been good at it. Another shocker.

His phone pinged with a text, and his heart sank.

Come talk?—Sara

He stood there, his head hung, unable to move.

"I'm so sorry, Noah," his sister said again. "I know how much you love Annabel."

Even *he* hadn't known just how much he loved that ten-pound little human until this moment. More than he'd ever realized.

Chapter Three

Sara was sitting in the kitchen of the foreman's cabin, thinking, thinking, thinking, when the tap came on the front door.

"It's me," Noah called out.

How was it possible that his voice still had the power to send goose bumps up her arms, make her feel such anticipation? No matter what she'd been going through as a kid, as a teenager, the sound of Noah Dawson's voice…

"Come on in," she said, standing up, then sitting down. Why had she told him to come back so soon? Maybe she wasn't quite ready after all.

It felt funny inviting him into his own home, but what about any of this didn't feel surreal?

Like the fact that Sara had spent the last fifteen minutes—with Annabel napping in her carrier beside her brother—working over the idea in her head.

Good idea? Bad idea? Her only option?

Was she really hoping to count on Noah Dawson?

She was in dire straits. Nowhere to go, very little money suddenly, and two babies to care for.

And Noah had clearly changed these past two years. Reopening the Dawson Family Guest Ranch had always been his dream. He'd made it happen. And he'd taken very good care of Annabel the past seven weeks. According to Daisy, he'd done 90 percent of that on his own. Daisy had helped out, and a couple times he'd called their old sitter, Mrs. Pickles, whose real name no one could even remember at this point, when he'd had emergencies he had to deal with on the ranch. But for the most part, Daisy said that Noah Dawson had been a full-time, hands-on father, Annabel in that Snugli as he'd directed the crew, made his phone calls, sent his emails, dealt with the invoices.

She heard the screen door open. "In the kitchen," she called out.

And then there he was. For a moment, she couldn't take her eyes off him. Earlier, when she'd first arrived, she'd barely been able to think, let alone focus on the fact that she had been reunited with Noah Dawson after two years. Now, his presence in the cabin was almost overwhelming.

This was the man she'd loved her whole life. The tall, sexy cowboy she'd never stopped thinking about. The person who'd taken care of her daughter for the past seven weeks, despite being a single rancher reopening the family business and clearly having a lot on his plate.

Noah had believed the baby was his, and he'd stepped up. Of course, Sara would take Annabel to Chance's pediatrician and have her fully examined, but her daughter looked healthy and happy and alert. Noah had done a good job.

She could hardly believe it. Noah Dawson.

Annabel started fussing, her eyes opening and fighting to close. Her little face turned red and scrunched up a bit, and Sara's heart leaped as she stood to go pick her up.

"May I?" he asked, gesturing toward Annabel.

No. She's mine.

The instinct was so strong that Sara instantly felt guilty. "She's only napped for about thirty-five minutes."

Sara wanted to go to her baby girl. *She knows her mother now and wants her mama.*

That was what Sara wanted to believe, anyway.

Noah might feel very differently. Like that Annabel sensed her daddy was back and wanted to be held by him. Noah was the only father Annabel had ever known.

Oh God. She hadn't really thought about that until this moment.

Suddenly, her idea, either good or bad, seemed like the *only* idea, the best plan for right now.

"Sure," Sara said.

Noah smiled and knelt down in front of the carrier, unbuckling the harness and taking Annabel out. She watched the way he carefully cradled Annabel against him, gently rocking her, and she knew this was not the same man she'd left two years ago.

That Noah Dawson was in there, she was sure. But a new one had emerged. The one who was about to make her cry with how loving he was being to the baby girl, how tender, the care he was showing in how he held her, cooed to her, rocked her.

"Her eyes are shutting," Noah said. "There's a baby swing she loves in the living room. Can you go grab it for me?"

She popped up, relieved to have something to do, somewhere to go other than sitting right there and staring at Noah Dawson in wonder. She went into the living room and got the swing and carried it to the kitchen. She set it beside Chance's carrier; he was still sleeping.

Noah knelt down again and laid Annabel in the swing, her eyes slightly opening. He pressed Gentle Sway, and the swing began moving lightly, the softest of lullabies playing from the side speakers. The baby's eyes closed.

He touched a finger to her cheek, then looked at Chance for a moment, smiling so sweetly at her son that her eyes almost welled up. She was insanely hormonal. Willem had never looked at Chance that way, with that kind of tenderness, awe. Her late husband had only looked at his son as the trophy heir.

Yes, her idea was a good one. Not just for her and Noah. But for the twins' sake.

Noah stood up and walked over to the coffee maker. He switched out the decaf and brewed a cup. "Can I get you anything?"

"I had coffee with Daisy. I'm fine for now."

"She told me," he said. "We were talking by the gate until you texted."

There was so much to say, but she didn't want to say any of it. She just wanted to sit here and not talk.

"They're both asleep now," he said with a nod toward the twins.

She glanced at them, then back at him. "You really seem to know what you're doing when it comes to babies. I'm very impressed, Noah."

She caught the way he glanced at her—the "when it comes to babies" hanging in the air as if he didn't know what he was doing in every other regard. Of course she didn't think that was true. Before Noah had started going a little too wild, heading down a road like his father had taken, he'd still been a good person, someone she could turn to. Steady. Trustworthy. Someone she could *always* count on. Until she gradually couldn't.

"I had to," he said. "I thought I was her father. Thank God for YouTube," he added.

She smiled. "I watched a few videos myself those first few days. Took me a while to get a good burp out of Chance. I'd been afraid to pat him too hard. Turns out I was way too gentle."

"Been there, learned that," he said with a nod, his gaze going to Chance. "Is Chance a family name?"

She shook her head. "It's a nickname I gave him the moment he was placed on my chest since I couldn't imagine calling him by his given name— Bancroft."

Noah rolled his eyes and she had to smile. "Willem's idea, I presume."

"His late mother's maiden name. I wanted to name him after my father, but he insisted that Preston wasn't stately enough." She shook her head. "If I could go back…"

"You had no choice but to marry Perry," he said. "Even I understand that. Barely, but I do. Your father was diagnosed with stage-two cancer when he had no health insurance. The bills took your savings, and then there was no way to pay for treatment when he needed to start radiation."

She felt tears well in her eyes. It meant so much that he *did* understand, that he didn't judge her. "I didn't realize how awful a person Willem was." She told him what was in the letter that Willem had written.

Noah's expression went from shock to horror to disgust. "Well, his sickening plan failed." He shook his head. "I'd like to scream every nasty thought I'm having about him from the rooftops, but I'll control myself because of these two," he added with a nod toward the twins. "I'd prefer never to hear his name again."

Exactly her thoughts since the lawyer's office. "Same here," she said.

She'd once really believed that Willem had loved her. He'd chased her all through high school, even though he was the town golden boy and she was the motherless daughter of a guest-ranch foreman who lived in the staff cabin she was in right now. Willem had truly seemed crazy about her—he listened when she spoke, told her interesting stories about his family, but she noticed the demeaning way he spoke to people, and she didn't like it. Besides, she'd *loved* Noah Dawson back then, and no one could ever compare.

Noah had been a wild child with a streak of good, and they'd been best friends since they were little. He'd always told her she was crazy for wanting him as a boyfriend and went for girls in his own circle instead, girls who skipped school and flashed boys in the hallway. Part of her always thought she'd dodged a bullet, but when they'd finally gotten together— for about six months—two years ago, when he had a small ranch of his own and was trying hard, she thought she'd help bring out the Noah Dawson who'd always been there. That was a mistake she'd made over and over, thinking people could change. They didn't, really. Maybe they could go a few degrees this way or that, but the core? That was settled. She understood that now.

So when Noah was sabotaging his fresh start on the ranch he'd wanted so bad, sabotaging their fledgling relationship, and then Willem Perry had started asking her out again, listening as she cried about Noah, about her sick father who would die without treatment, she'd let Willem take her away from her troubles. He'd promised her the moon, that he'd take care of her dad, and all he wanted in return was the woman of his dreams: her. She'd fallen for it all.

But what she'd really been was a notch. A conquest Willem had never been able to make until she'd been totally desperate. And the truth behind that made him resentful. And mean.

Just when things were so bad that she planned to leave her husband, determined to find a way to continue her dad's medical care, she found out she was pregnant—with twins. The news, for a while, turned things around; for a few weeks, Willem was kinder, until that changed too. He'd accused her of cheating with Noah, had gotten paranoid the twins weren't his. A prenatal DNA test confirmed they were Willem's, but his mind had gone twisted. He'd threatened her every time she told him she was leaving, and once, when she had left him, he sent a lawyer after her who scared the hell out of her that she'd lose custody of the babies entirely. She'd gone back home numb, not sure what she was going to do, how she'd get away from him and not lose her children. Then her father died, and she'd been too grief-stricken to even think about Willem.

All that was in the past, including her husband. The very recent past with lessons she'd not soon forget.

Noah came over to the table with a steaming mug of coffee. He sat down across from her, and again, she was overwhelmed by how close he was.

"Before I came here," she said, "I'd just heard from Willem's lawyer that you'd restored the guest ranch and are reopening this weekend. I immediately noticed the new signs on the road leading to the turn and the huge sign on the shiny gates. The landscaping, the foreman's cabin, the barn—you've done an amazing job. A lot of the place looks even better than when I lived here."

He smiled. "Thanks. Wait till you see the farmhouse, the cabins, barns, the pastures and the trails. We still have work to do, but the heavy lifting is done."

A wistfulness crept into her expression, her gaze moving around the kitchen. "It feels so good to be back here."

"That's how I felt when I first came home. My brothers, not so much. But I guess for some of us, roots have a grip, even when they're a tangled mess."

She nodded, her gaze shifting to the napping babies.

"I guess after we talk," he said, "you're getting back in that Range Rover and I'll never see any of you again."

There's your in, she thought. Good idea, bad idea,

whichever—right now it was all she had. "Actually, quite the opposite, if you're open to my idea."

"What idea is that?" he asked, his eyes intense on her.

"I need a job and a place to stay," she said. "I'll work for you for room and board and a reasonable salary so I can get on my feet. There's a lot I can do on the ranch."

He looked at her like she'd grown an extra head. "You married one of the richest men in Wyoming. Selling that Range Rover alone could set you up for a while."

"He left me with nothing," she explained. "Chance inherits the bulk of the estate when he's twenty-one. I have fourteen days to vacate my house, and anything that isn't clothing or personal jewelry stays. I don't even want to go back there, knowing now what that monster did." She squeezed her eyes shut. "My dad's gone—and I'm alone. Except for my children. *Children*," she repeated, her voice breaking. "Look at what I have now. *Both* babies. I just need some time and a way to get back on my own two feet."

The emotion that settled on his face looked a lot like relief. "Of course I'll hire you," he said. "Anything you need, Sara. Always."

That same relief now flooded her. Okay. She had a safe place to land with her infants. She had a job.

She had everything that was familiar and comforting. She'd be okay. This *had* been a good idea.

"Thank you, Noah."

He nodded and looked out the window as if regrouping. "I won't lose Annabel," he whispered, and he glanced back at her so fast she realized he hadn't meant to say it aloud. He picked up his mug and took a sip of his coffee. "I turned the spare room into her nursery," he quickly said, "so that's already all set up. You could take the guest room, and she and Chance can share the nursery. It's small, but hey, so are they."

"I'd prefer that to taking a room in the farmhouse. This cabin will always feel like home."

He glanced at her with such warmth in his eyes that she wanted to fling her arms around him and just hold him—for old times, for now. As a link to tomorrow and the next few weeks and months. But touching Noah Dawson had always gotten her in trouble in every way, and she had to rely on him enough right now—she wasn't going to mix up nostalgia, being grateful and need with anything else.

And anyway, she recalled that his grandparents had always kept two of the bedrooms of the main house available for emergencies regarding guests. Family members in arguments. Couples breaking up overnight. Plumbing issues. Right now, Daisy had a room and she'd need one for a nursery, so that left only two. It wouldn't be right to ask for one.

"I'm so used to Annabel being here," Noah said. "Honestly, I never thought she'd be going anywhere except when she graduated from high school."

She stared at him. "You really committed to being her father, huh."

He nodded. "I love that little girl. And I'll love her twin too. I want you all right here. Besides, the guest room is your old bedroom."

She did like the idea of staying in her old room. And she couldn't deny that Annabel looked happy and well cared for. *And* Noah had definitely turned the Dawson Family Guest Ranch around. But she didn't trust him—aside from knowing he'd never mean her harm. He'd taken her trust two years ago by sabotaging everything he held dear, including their relationship. Then her husband had obliterated what little faith she had left in people. She couldn't count on anyone but herself, and that was just the way it was. She'd do what she had to in order to fill a bank account with enough money to get back on her feet, then she'd figure out where she'd go from there. Maybe she'd leave Wyoming—not that could she could imagine it.

She'd go back to the house in Wellington tomorrow to collect her things, everything that was hers. Then she'd officially move to the ranch with the twins and start over. She could breathe here, make a plan here. Being a foreman's daughter meant she had ranch life in her blood and bones; she'd been assistant forewoman at the last ranch she'd worked at before she'd gotten married.

"Glad to have you at Dawson Family Guest Ranch, Sara," he said, extending his hand. "We can talk about what position you'd like once you're settled. I could use an experienced assistant, if you're interested. But there are a few open positions—from leading children's activities and workshops to being a cowgirl."

She nodded, so relieved at how this had all worked out. "I'm glad to be here."

He had no idea how glad she was. This had always been home. And now, for the time being anyway, it would be again. She'd get on her feet, figure things out and then off she'd go.

But Noah hadn't let go of her hand, and she wasn't pulling it away. Their history, their past, good and bad, lingered heavy in the air between them. There was *too* much to talk about, and right now, she just wanted to gaze at Annabel and get back the last seven weeks.

But then Annabel started fussing again, and Noah reached for her, then put up his hands and stepped back. "Old habits," he said. "I guess I don't have to jump anymore."

"It'll be an absolute treat to care for her," she said, holding the baby girl, who once again was struggling to keep her eyes open. "Something I'll never take for granted that I get to do after all."

He nodded and reached out a hand to hers, giving it a gentle squeeze. "Maybe we can put them both down in her crib, and then I can fill you in on the last seven weeks."

"Sounds good," she said, snuggling Annabel close, aware that Noah was watching her.

As he lifted Chance's carrier—the little guy was still fast asleep—she couldn't help but wonder what was going to happen, how this would all go. Could she and Noah share a cabin with all that had happened between them? Would the past flare up? Or would they both just ignore it?

She would definitely ignore it, she told herself. *No matter what he reminds you of or makes you think about, no matter how comforting it would be to be in his arms. Ignore it.*

This was her fresh start, her chance for a new life. Two precious little beings depended on her now, and she would *not* let them down.

"Oh, what a lovely room," Sara said, looking all around the nursery as they walked inside, each holding a carrier. She'd stopped in her tracks, her mouth slightly open as though she wasn't expecting this.

Noah realized that she'd probably been expecting the basics. Not a room fit for a...beloved baby daughter. "It helped that I couldn't sleep the past several weeks, between Annabel waking up every few hours and constantly worrying about something or other about the ranch or if I'd forgotten to take care of something. Made it easy to find the extra hours to turn this room into something special for her. Now them," he added, nodding at Chance.

He watched as Sara spun slowly, taking in the furnishings. The white spindle crib with the pastel monkey sheets. The stars and moon mobile that hung overhead and played lullabies. The white floor lamp that he'd stenciled matching stars and moons on. The big braided rug in yellows and pinks and blues. The yellow glider that he'd practically lived in the past seven weeks. The white dresser topped with the changing pad and basket of diapers and ointments. The bookcase he'd filled with board books and baby books and lined with stuffed animals. And the window with the yellow velvet drapes, tree branches and leaves and blue sky the view.

Every time Noah came in here, he felt so strongly that this was all meant to be—that Annabel was meant to be here. The first few days, his sister had

asked if he was worried about splitting his time between fatherhood and getting the final details taken
care of for the grand reopening, then less than two
months away, and for reasons he couldn't quite ever
figure out, the answer was more no than yes. Everything about Annabel in his life had felt so right, his
bond with her so immediate, that he'd simply made
it work. That was what you did.

He hadn't done it with Sara two years ago. Or
with the small ranch he'd tried to keep going. That
was what he'd thought about long and hard once he'd
gotten his act together five months ago and became
the person she'd wanted him to be then. Why had
he let her go? Why?

He didn't know. And he hated thinking about it.

"Thank you for taking such good care of her,"
Sara whispered. "For giving her this beautiful home
and nursery."

He managed a smile. He almost wished she'd stop
reminding him that Annabel wasn't his. That was
unfair; he knew it. But still.

This was going to be hard. However this new arrangement was going to go, what would happen. It
would be hard. He had no doubt about it.

"How about if I put Chance down," she said, carefully taking her son from the carrier, "since I'm used

to transferring him when he's asleep, and you put Annabel down?"

"Good idea," he said, reaching for Annabel and cuddling her close for a moment before dropping a kiss to her soft little head. *Love you, baby girl*, he said silently.

The moment she touched the soft sheets with the tiny pastel monkeys, she stopped fussing and her eyes closed.

He sighed inwardly with relief again. His baby girl wasn't leaving. He wasn't losing Annabel.

Thank you, universe.

"This is home for her," Sara whispered, her voice shaky. "Of course she likes her crib."

He eyed Sara, wishing he could take her in his arms and just hold her, comfort her. This had to be so damned hard for *her* on so many levels. "And luckily, Chance seems like a champion napper who can sleep anywhere," he said with a gentle smile.

She nodded, her face brightening a bit. "He's good that way." But her face fell a moment later. He knew her well enough to be able to tell she was suffering from regret-itis. Wishing things had been different, that she'd been with Annabel from the moment she'd been born.

"Hey. She's your daughter, Sara. And she'll be napping in your arms like she's been there from moment one in no time."

"How'd you know that was…" She trailed off and turned away.

"I've known you forever, Sara. Remember? Nothing escapes me about you."

She glanced at him, then gave a slow nod, and he wondered if he was getting too personal, if he should be more professional now, since they were going to work together. Heck, he was going to be her boss. "I guess we can leave them to nap and go talk," she said.

"I have a weird craving for a grilled cheese sandwich," he said. "Want one?"

"Actually, yes. An hour ago I couldn't imagine ever eating again. Now I'm starved."

Because your life is back on track, he thought. *You feel okay*. He hoped she did, anyway.

They headed down to the kitchen, and he told her to sit, that he had it. In minutes, she was sniffing the air appreciatively.

"Grilled cheese was always my comfort food," she said with a soft smile. "Whenever I was upset, if I couldn't sleep at midnight, my dad would make me a grilled cheese and I'd feel better. I think a lot had to do with him making it for me and sitting next to me at this very table while I took a few bites that made me feel so much better."

"Yup," he said. His closest-in-age brothers had been like that for him when there had been overlap with them staying on the ranch as he'd grown up. "And I'm not surprised Annabel conked out so easily. Meeting her mama was big stuff."

"It's only seven weeks, right?" she said, her voice shaky. "That's nothing."

She'd inadvertently thrown him a solid right hook in the stomach. Seven weeks had been more than enough for him to develop a serious bond with Annabel. Then again, he'd developed that bond within days. The weeks passing had just cemented it, his love for that baby growing every day. "A blip, Sara," he forced himself to say. "And you're together now. That's all that matters anymore."

"I'm glad she's staying here—for your sake too," she said.

"I'm not gonna lie. I'm very relieved. But I'm happiest for Annabel. I hope you know that. I love that baby. Truly love her, as if she were my own. I'd rather she had her mother and a twin brother and that she knew who she truly was than lived a lie with me for who knows how long."

And that was the truth, no matter how he felt about Annabel. If he loved that baby, he wanted what was best for her, not what was best for himself.

He thought about the letter Sara told him Willem had left for her. What if the rat bastard *hadn't* been reckless with that stupid Porsche? What if he

had lived to ninety-three like his just-as-awful father had? Sara would never have known her daughter. He would never have known who'd left Annabel.
All their stories would be very different.

"I believe that," she said. "You always had a big
heart."

Again, so much of their past hung heavy in the
air, regrets and good times. He'd let her down—hard.
Driven her right into Willem's arms. He'd never for-
give himself for that.

"Why do you think he left her here?" he asked.
"With a note saying she was mine?"

"Probably to create havoc for you, mess up your
carefree bachelor's life, screw up your good thing
with the reopening of the ranch, if he even knew
about that. Was there press about the grand reopening? He must have read it."

Noah nodded. "The *Bear Ridge Daily* did a big
story on it. So did the Converse County paper."

"I think he thought he was getting the last laugh,"
Sara said. "He knew how I felt about you and he
couldn't stand it, even when I told him that was in
the past. He never believed me. He resented you and
probably thought it was sweet justice that you'd think
the baby he didn't want was yours."

He wondered how she felt about him now. Two
years ago, after a drinking bender that had left Noah
in no condition to drive her and her dad to his ap-

pointment at the county hospital since her car was in the shop, she'd screamed that she was done with him, then had sent him a text a few hours later: I'll never be done with you, Noah. Even if we never see or speak to each other again, I'll always wish you well in my heart. But goodbye.

Two weeks later, he'd heard she'd married the rat bastard.

He had a feeling he'd never be clear on why he'd screwed up with Sara once he'd finally allowed himself to be in a relationship with her. He'd had everything, and he'd let it all go. Sara. His starter ranch. He'd frittered away most of the savings account she wouldn't take from him on really dumb track bets. Then he had what he'd supposedly wanted, according to his sister, who'd eventually staged an intervention with his brothers: nothing.

"Well, I'm glad Willem chose me," he said. "Mine or not, it was an honor to take care of her the past seven weeks, Sara. Two years ago, I couldn't have done it. Two months ago, I did. I'm a different person now, if you haven't noticed."

"I noticed." She opened her mouth as if to say something else but apparently decided against it. He imagined she'd been about to say: *It's a start, anyway. Let's see where you are in six months. Or a year. Maybe you're one challenge away from messing it all up again.*

He could see in her face that she didn't trust him, and he didn't blame her. But things *were* different now—because he trusted *himself.* That was everything. He hadn't known anything about that two years ago or five years ago or ever. But when he'd taken on reopening the ranch, when his sister and brothers had told him he'd hit rock bottom and there was only one way to go from there, he'd grabbed control of his life with both hands. His siblings had believed in him when they'd had no reason to, when he himself had no reason to. By the time Annabel had been left on his porch, he truly was a changed man.

Sara leaned against the doorway frame, crossing her arms over her chest, her long brown ponytail falling against her neck. "What a mess this could have been had he left her with strangers. I could have had a custody fight on my hands for my own daughter."

"The universe was looking out for you all along," he said, lifting up an edge of the grilled cheese to see if it was golden brown. It was. He was surprised the conversation hadn't distracted him into burning down the entire kitchen.

"I think so." She nodded. "Wow, that looks good," she said, her gaze on the grilled cheese sandwiches.

"And here it comes, good old-fashioned comfort food," he said, putting the plates on the small round table by the window and grabbing two raspberry seltzers from the fridge.

"Thanks, Noah. I have a feeling I'll be saying that a lot."

"Sure beats the alternative," he said, then regretted it. She'd had some choice words for him back then. He didn't want to remind her of bad times. He wasn't that guy anymore.

But she gave him a smile and picked up half her sandwich. "I was wondering if I could borrow your pickup truck today. When the babies wake up, I can drive over to my house—my former house—and get Chance's things. Then I'll be done with that place."

He cracked open his seltzer. "I'll do you one better. I'll drive you and help you cart everything. And how about if we ask Daisy to watch the twins?"

Sara frowned. "I hate the thought of leaving Annabel for even a second when I just got her back."

"We could take the twins along if you prefer, but it would be a lot easier and faster to get the job done without having to worry about them or check on them."

She nodded. "You're right. And Daisy does seem to adore Annabel. Think she'd mind?"

"Mind? Annabel's her—" He clamped his mouth shut.

"Niece," she said solemnly. "Annabel sure had a lot of love here. I'm grateful. Your brothers too?"

He shook his head. "They know about her, but they all said they'd never step foot on the ranch again, that it was my thing and they were glad Daisy was here because it made them feel less guilty. I think a few of them were worried the baby news would trip me up about the ranch. I'm pretty sure they're all waiting to see how things shake down. No doubt Daisy fills them in."

She nodded. "Your sister can still be Aunt Daisy," she said, taking another bite of her sandwich. "He who won't be named and I were both only children. Annabel can use an aunt and four uncles."

He smiled. "And Daisy is six months pregnant and wants baby experience. She's loved her babysitting time with Annabel these past weeks. She's an old pro already. I'm sure she'd be happy to watch both."

"Okay, then. I'll take you up on the offer for help and your sister as babysitter."

He nodded and picked up his sandwich and took a bite. He'd eaten plenty of grilled cheeses here as a kid, just as Sara had had many meals in the main house. They'd been inseparable as children, the same age, when his five siblings had all been older and not so interested in the sprout tagging along. His eldest brother, Ford, was six years older, just a little more than a year separating all of them. They had three mothers among them. Daisy and Noah with the third wife. Axel, Rex and Zeke with the second, and Ford with the first Mrs. Dawson.

"Thank you again, Noah," Sara said, placing her hand on his. "For lunch. For the relief of a home and a job. For taking such good care of my daughter."

I'd do anything for you, he wanted to say, and it felt true, but when he'd needed to step up, he'd failed her. Gunk he didn't want to think about anymore but often kept him awake at night. For two years.

So he just nodded and squeezed her hand, then picked up his phone and called his sister.

A half hour later, Daisy was up in the nursery with the twins, happy to watch Annabel and Chance for however long they needed, and he and Sara were in his truck alone, heading down the drive until he realized they forgot about the Range Rover.

New plan. He'd follow her in the truck so she could return the fancy SUV to the house where it belonged, since the car, like everything else, was apparently in Perry's name.

Now he was behind her on the freeway, so aware of her in the silver SUV, never wanting to let her out of his sight again.

Chapter Four

Thanks to Noah's help, Sara got Chance's stuff and her clothing and toiletries and some personal items out of the Wellington house and into the pickup in under an hour—including the double infant stroller that Willem must have moved to a closet in the garage and then forgotten about. He'd gotten rid of the extras of everything they'd bought two of—a baby swing, a crib. The stroller was the only sign in the house that she'd been expecting twins.

Part of her wanted to leave it, but she'd picked out the stroller herself, knowing she'd be the one using it 99 percent of the time, drawn to the soft blue and white color. *It doesn't offend*, Willem had said when she'd shown him the online photo, so she'd ordered it. Ugh, that had been Willem's favorite description. *It offends*, he'd say about the most innocuous things.

She shivered as memory after memory hit her. *Just finish up and get out of here*, she told herself.

The shortest time possible spent in this house, the better. The three-story white Colonial with the black shutters and red door was classic and beautiful on the outside, and as cold and austere as a walk-in freezer on the inside. The walls were all the same cool gray, the furnishings white, black or cream. Willem had found color—and a whole host of other things—tacky. Since he'd passed away, out of Willem-ingrained habit she'd straightened the throw pillows if she'd sat on the sofa and shifted all the hand towels in the bathroom so they were perfectly aligned. More than once, Willem had called her upstairs as though something awful had happened and he'd point out that the shampoo and conditioner containers needed to face front, not one of them sideways or show evidence that they'd been squeezed with depressions in the center.

She'd lived like that for two years. And had lost her father anyway.

She'd tried, given it her all, done whatever it had taken to try to save her dad. Preston Mayhew had loved life and had been raring to go, to fight the traitorous cells with everything he had. She'd been given an extra year and a half with him. When he was first diagnosed, he'd told her he'd be fine with sticking around long enough to walk her down the aisle even with a cane, and the pure joy on his face when he'd done just that had let her know he'd go at peace, assured his only child would be okay without him in the world.

She had to get out of this house. "I think that's it," she said to Noah.

She'd sped through her bedroom, the room she'd shared with Willem, where she'd given birth, where her husband had tried very hard to take something precious from her. She'd been unable to look at the bed or the pretty chair where the midwife had sat beside her for hours during labor, so encouraging, so kind. Granted, Sara hadn't gotten to know the midwife, Katherine, all that well, but she could only assume the woman was racked with guilt and unable to live with herself, no matter how much Willem had paid her off, no matter how desperate she'd been. What she'd done was reprehensible. Sara couldn't imagine any amount of money making what she'd done even a serious consideration. She'd have to deal with the midwife soon. Very soon. What if she was planning to assist with another birth? Sara would call the lawyer tomorrow and discuss it all.

Her stomach turning over, Sara pushed all that away, focusing on the man watching her right now. She let herself drink in the sight of him, so different from Willem. Noah was over six feet by a couple inches at least, lanky and muscular with warm, deep blue eyes and a mop of shaggy dark hair that curled by his nape. Movie-star hair straight from the shower or bed. He was incredibly sexy—objectively speaking. Women had always buzzed around Noah. Willem had been attractive but not sexy, tall and stocky with pin-straight light blond hair and ice-blue eyes that neither twin had inherited. They both had her coloring. Was it awful that she was grateful she didn't see him in them? Grateful as she was to have them.

She stopped in front of the fireplace mantel, chills running up her spine, and then walked past, leaving the framed photographs there.

Noah nodded at the mantel. "Not taking any?"

There weren't many, since Willem had also thought it was tacky to have personal photographs all over the place. She'd always loved the idea of stairway walls lined with family pictures, but the stairway wall was blank, a cold gray like the rest of the house.

"I really don't want them," she said.

He plucked their wedding photo off the mantel. "The twins might one day," he said gently. He looked at the framed photograph and shook his head. "Perry's expression says you're his trophy. Is that what it was like? He finally got the girl?"

"Yup. It was more about the conquest than anything. Then he resented me for it."

"I'm sorry you went through all that, Sara. All of it. I wish I could have helped with your dad."

"Well, you tried," she said.

When she'd told him how bleak the situation was, that the hospital couldn't continue with treatment because of the lack of insurance and lack of payment on the last bill, Noah had handed her a check that she knew was the contents of his bank accounts—business and personal. It meant he'd lose his small ranch that he'd wanted so badly, and the gesture touched and unsettled her. He'd give up his dream to help her, but the amount, generous as it was, would pay only the last bill and barely begin to cover the month ahead. He'd lose his ranch and she wouldn't be able to keep up with the payments anyway. It was lose-lose, and so she'd turned it down. That was the first night they'd made love, when they'd tried to be a couple, but it was all too much for him. The intimacy, she thought. Just too much. Within a few months he clearly couldn't handle it and so he began acting out in ways it took her a while to catch onto. By then it was too late for them. She'd ended their relationship after only six months together and started dating Willem, who'd actually seemed like a breath of fresh air.

Ha. Not that it was funny in the slightest.

Her phone pinged with a text. It was from Holton, Willem's attorney.

Hope I'm not overstepping but please advise re: the female twin.

She texted back, Alive and well. We'll all be okay.

Wonderful news, Sara. Also, I checked into the midwife's license. According to the Wyoming Board of Nursing, she allowed her license of thirty-seven years to expire just this month without renewing, and local hospitals and OBs that I checked with let me know she called them to say she had officially retired. At least she's out of business.

Sara shivered.

It was something, but not enough. She'd have to deal with the midwife at some point soon. But for right now, when she walked out the door of this house, she'd close this chapter of her life. She'd never want to hear the lawyer's name or her late husband's again. There was too much to process right now, too much to adjust to or she'd storm the midwife's home with the sheriff in tow. Or maybe just knock on the woman's door and find out what the hell Willem had threatened her with or what dire straits she'd been in to agree to such a heinous act. When the time felt right, she would do just that.

Forcing those thoughts away right now, Sara took the photo out of Noah's hand and put it back on the mantel. "I plan to legally change Chance's name from Bancroft Perry to Chance Mayhew since I'll be taking back my maiden name."

"What do you think you'll rename Annabel?"

Sara held his gaze. "I can't tell you how touched I was when I found out you named her Annabel. *My* middle name. Unless that was a coincidence? You just happened to like the name?"

"Well, I do happen to, but it was no coincidence. You were always my best friend, Sara, no matter what. And I guess I wanted her to have a piece of the best woman I know. Who knew she had *all* of you?"

She smiled, the urge to hug him so strong. She forced herself to stay put. "I think Annabel is perfect for her. Annabel Mayhew, it is."

"I got a lot right with her. Don't know how, but I did. Gives me hope for the ranch."

"I believe in you, Noah. Always have."

"I know," he said, looking down, and she could tell a little of that old Noah was still there, the guy who couldn't handle too much emotional honesty without getting itchy or wanting to run.

She'd do him a solid and change the subject. "For the twins, for someday," she said, "I'll take one photo album that has an array of photos from when Willem and I first started dating to when we brought Chance home." She shivered. "But how will I explain why there are no photos of Annabel the day they were born?"

She burst into tears and covered her face with her hands, and Noah wrapped his arms around her. She'd been holding on, but it was the thing that whacked her legs out from under her. The idea of her children having questions she'd hate to answer.

"You have lots of time to figure out those details," he said, his arms tightening around her. "Right now, let's focus on what's necessary. Like getting the hell out of here."

He tightened his hold for just a second, and oh God, did that feel good. She let herself sag against him, needing this, his comfort, his strength, all their beautiful history like air right now.

But she couldn't need him this way. It was too, too much. She wiped at her eyes and pulled away, slightly embarrassed at falling apart, but then again, this was Noah Dawson, who'd seen her through just about all the rough times of her life.

And she couldn't lie to herself. Being in his arms again felt even better than she'd expected. Maybe because he had changed. Or maybe because she'd missed him so damned much. Either way, she had to be careful with how she responded to him. She had leaned on someone for the last time. Now, she'd only lean on herself.

"I almost forgot," Noah said as he drove down the freeway in his pickup, Sara's Range Rover left behind with her old life. "My dad left you something in his will."

Sara had had enough of wills and surprises. She couldn't even summon the polite words to feign interest so she just turned toward him.

"A garden plot behind the foreman's cabin," he said. "Apparently it was your mother's once?"

A spark of joy lit inside Sara, a warmth as memories rushed over her. Sara as a little girl kneeling in the grass in front of the wood-framed raised garden bed, her mother letting her drop in the seeds as she explained about vegetables you planted in the warmer weather, like tomatoes and green peppers.

"It was added to the letter he left me," Noah said.

"'Tell Sara I bequeath her the garden plot behind the foreman's cabin. Her mother built it and grew all kinds of vegetables. Sara was a nice gal, so I wanted to leave her something.'"

"I can't tell you how moved I am," she said. "That is really kind, Noah."

He nodded. "My dad had his moments, didn't he? You should have seen the letter he wrote me. I cried for a minute straight. I seriously couldn't stop."

She looked at him. "Really? What did the letter say?"

"That he was sorry for ruining our family legacy and everything his parents had built and dreamed of. That he was sorry for letting us down. He said he owned the ranch outright, and the land, never sold any part of it, and he'd always paid his property taxes, even if he let the place fall apart."

Sara had been leveled by what his father had done to the place, how he'd slowly destroyed it. The final straw for her dad as foreman had been the afternoon that Noah's dad had drunkenly smashed his truck into the barn next to their cabin—though luckily her and her dad's horses were in the pasture and not injured. Bo Dawson had refused to pay for the repairs to the barn and left it as it was. Between not paying his bills, storm damage he wouldn't take care of, and time, the old word of mouth had spread, and

guests stopped coming completely. Out of respect for
Noah's late grandparents, her dad had stayed on for
a few weeks more, trying to do what he could and
reason with Noah's father, but the man was beyond
hope, and they'd left. That was twelve years ago.

"He still cared about Dawson Family Guest
Ranch," Sara said. "Even if he didn't show it or have
the wherewithal to do anything about it. The place
itself meant something to him."

Noah nodded. "I used to think actions spoke
louder than anything, and I've come to realize what
people do masks all kinds of things they can't say
or articulate."

She supposed that was true. Nothing was ever
really black-and-white. She'd known that Noah had
cared about her even when he was letting her down.
People were complicated. Life was complicated. If
anyone had told her five years ago that one day she'd
be trapped in an emotionally abusive marriage, unsure how to get herself and Chance safely away, she
never would have believed it. She would have smugly
said she'd never *be* in such a marriage to begin with,
let alone not be able to get out.

"My dad went on to say in the letter that he hoped
I'd take charge of the place," Noah said, thankfully
shaking her out of her thoughts. "That I'd reopen the
Dawson Family Guest Ranch even on a small scale,

that he felt awful he couldn't leave any money to make that happen. But that he knew I was the Dawson to do it. He said I had a streak of him running in my veins but more of my grandparents in me, and he was sure I'd reopen the place and have my grandparents smiling down at me and the ranch."

"Wow," she said, marveling at how people *could* surprise you. "To all of it."

He nodded. "He left us all letters. At the will reading after the funeral, I was the only one who shared my letter. My siblings wouldn't. Even Daisy, and she was never all that private, especially with me."

"What do you think he wrote in your siblings' letters?" she asked. "I mean, if he envisioned you reopening the ranch, what else was there?"

"Nothing as far as I know. He got so broke at the end that he even sold the chipped dishes and cheap silverware. I can't even imagine what he wrote in their letters. But whatever he did write had an impact, since they're all so tight-lipped about it."

"They invested in reopening the ranch," she added. "And they invested in you too. So he must have made some kind of amends."

He nodded. "They refuse to step foot on the property, though. Except Daisy. And only because she's pregnant and seems to be completely on her own."

"She's got you," Sara said. "And me."

He glanced at her. "I'm glad for that."

They were quiet for a few moments, the only sound the rush of the tires as they drove down the freeway.

"You know what's interesting?" she said. "That the last person you expected to change your life ended up doing just that. Your father."

He nodded. "I spent a lot of time thinking about exactly that as I was working on the ranch. My siblings and I had given up on him completely the last few years." He sucked in a breath. "I hate wishing I could go back. At the time, I felt justified in leaving him to his own destruction. We all did. He constantly told us to get lost and mind our own business, that it was his property and we were trespassing. So we stopped badgering him after a while. Once the drinking got really bad and he almost ran over Ford one morning, dead drunk at 10:00 a.m., we left him alone."

"I know all about wishing you could go back, Noah. I guess we just do the best we can at the time with what we know, what we believe is true and right."

He glanced at her and nodded. "I would have let you know about the garden plot, but I wasn't sure about getting in touch. I couldn't imagine you driving an hour a few times a week to tend to a twelve-foot-by-six-foot garden bed."

"To get away from Willem for a few hours?" she said. "I would have."

He reached for her hand and squeezed it. "Well, it's yours now. And time to plant."

"Being back at the ranch when it looks the way it does now, being with you, my old friend, it almost feels like the world's been righted for me."

He turned to look at her, and his expression was full of so many different emotions. He squeezed her hand and then returned his attention to the road, and she wondered if she'd said too much again, made too much of their reunion. To change the subject, she remarked on how beautiful the Wyoming wilderness was in late May when the leaves bloomed and wildflowers spread their gorgeous color across the brown and green landscape, the still-snowcapped mountain range in the far distance. He agreed, and then they were silent the rest of the way home.

As Noah drove through the gates of the Dawson Family Guest Ranch and up the dirt road past the foreman's cabin, Sara took in the manicured but rustic grounds, pastures and fields and wilderness in every direction. There were cute wooden signs posted with arrows, miles and timing to get to the main house, the foreman's cabin, the cafeteria, the lodge, Bear Ridge Creek, riding trails and the trail system in the woods that were part of the ranch. Wildflowers were everywhere, and there were hunter green wooden benches, picnic tables and wooden swings hanging from tree branches. The ranch looked so welcoming and inviting.

"Did you hire people to help besides you and Daisy?" she asked as they drove past a pretty, rectangular log cabin painted a rustic white with a sign reading Guest Cafeteria. Picnic tables were out front.

"I have a good staff. For one, my grandparents' old cook, Cowboy Joe, agreed to come back and take the job. No one makes better burgers or omelets or barbecue than him. He's nearing seventy, but I hired him two helpers. The caf will be open from seven to eight thirty, twelve to one thirty, and five to six thirty for dinner. Cowboy Joe will handle breakfast and lunch, and Daisy wanted to take the dinner shift. She's also the guest relations manager."

"Perfect," she said. "So you'll focus on the ranch and she'll focus on the guests."

"Yup. I have a great team assembled—maintenance, housekeeping, cowboys and cowgirls. It's a small staff, but we're starting small. We're having a final staff meeting before opening day on Thursday morning—you can come to that and we'll get your role squared away beforehand. Memorial Day weekend and through the rest of next week, all six cabins are booked with a retreat. Something about getting your groove back."

Sara smiled. "Really?"

He shrugged. "Some kind of female empowerment thing. It's led by a life coach. She's bringing her own protein shake mixes."

Sara laughed. "Sounds great. And are there bookings beyond opening weekend?"

"Not all the cabins all the weeks or weekends, but so far, so good."

"I'm really happy for you, Noah. Looks like the ranch will be a big success."

"I hope so. I know a lot can go wrong."

She glanced at him and saw for the first time the worry in his expression. Everything must be riding on the opening, she realized. His dreams and future. His siblings' investment. What he wanted to carry on for his grandparents—and now even for his father.

As the main house where Noah grew up came into view, Sara's jaw almost dropped. Once peeling with a rotting foundation, the white clapboard farmhouse looked pristine and gleaming as it stood in the sunshine, a white wood–fenced pasture beside it and several trails through the low and high grasslands leading into the woods about a hundred feet away. The guest cabins, which couldn't be viewed from the dirt road that ended at the house, were between the foreman's cabin and the creek, nestled privately in the woods. Given what the main house looked like, she knew the cabins had to be beautifully restored too.

"You've done wonders with the place," she said. "And it'll take off. I believe that."

"Here's hoping so," he said, parking along the side of the house.

They headed up the porch steps, and he pulled open the screen door, Daisy coming over with Chance fast asleep in her arms.

"This guy got fussy a little while ago, so I walked around with him, rocking him a bit, and he fell back asleep. I couldn't bear to put him down. He's such a love bug." She breathed in the baby shampoo scent of him. "Ahhh. I know being a mom twenty-four-seven like I'll be in three months won't be all rockabye and baby shampoo goodness, but I don't care. I can't wait!"

Sara laughed. "Know what you're having?"

"I told the radiologist and my OB that I want to be surprised," she said. "Which was a surprise in itself, given that I've had enough of the unexpected lately for a lifetime."

Sara had a feeling Daisy was talking about the

father of her baby, and she was so curious, but until her old friend wanted to tell, she wouldn't ask.

"Where's my baby girl—" Noah said and then froze and turned to Sara. "Sorry. I mean, where's Annabel?" He smiled but looked so uncomfortable that suddenly Sara felt equally uncomfortable. How hard this must be for him, to have to step back from Annabel, to accept that she wasn't his baby after all.

His phone rang, and he seemed relieved for the interruption. He read something on the little screen. "Oh man. I've actually got to run. Hermione—one of the alpine goats—escaped her corral, and Dylan, one of our cowboys, is having a hard time getting her back."

Daisy laughed. "That Hermione is a wily one."

"See you in a few," Noah said, looking at his sister and then Sara before sprinting out.

"Annabel's napping in the kitchen," Daisy said. "I was just sitting at the table with the baby monitor on high volume making a list of all the things I'm going to need. Taking a peek inside the twins' baby bag helped me a lot. Taking care of two babies must feel like a huge change from just one."

"It is, but every time I look at Annabel, I almost can't believe she's real. That makes double the work a lot easier." She smiled. "And yup, sure is a lot of stuff," Sara said. "Of course for the past seven weeks, I didn't know I'd need two of everything after all."

Daisy shook her head. "I still can't process what happened. My ex—" She bit her lip. "He was this and that, but I don't think he'd ever do something like that. How *could* anyone?"

Sara felt her face fall. "It's the scariest thing, Daisy. That I didn't know what I was getting myself into. But it turns out I made a deal with the devil."

Daisy shook her head. "Don't do that to yourself. I remember you telling me how special Willem made you feel, how listened to, how important. Plus, he was instrumental in getting your dad the best care, Sara. He pulled the wool over your eyes with who he was, but he did help with your dad, so there's that. And there's also something else."

"The twins," Sara said, knowing what Daisy was doing. Letting her take herself off the hook. She put a hand on her friend's arm. "Thank you, Daisy."

Sara followed her friend into the kitchen, struck, as always, by how much she and her brother looked alike. Daisy had lighter hair—hers was a beautiful honey-brown—but they had the same blue eyes and gorgeous features. Though two years older, Daisy had always been warm and kind to Sara. When Sara had gotten her period for the first time, and her mother had been gone a year and half prior, it was Daisy she'd gone to, all nervous and worried and thrilled.

It was also Daisy she'd gone to about her first kiss and first crush, admitting it was on her brother Noah, which worried Daisy to no end, and under "no circumstances are you allowed to let him kiss you, let alone touch a piece of your clothing!" Sara had said she could only half promise, given that she was in love and only thirteen and driven by hormones and the brain of a teenager. She and Noah had been best friends, but he'd refused to date her, saying he didn't want to mess up the friendship, but she saw the girls he went for. C cups. High heels. Hips. She had none of those things. And then her father had told her they were moving when she was sixteen and that was that until Noah took a job as a cowboy on the new ranch her father managed and then moved there when he was eighteen. But he still wouldn't mess with their friendship.

That had gone on for years, and their romance had only lasted six months. No matter how helpful he was to her now, she'd never trust Noah Dawson with her heart again.

Sara saw Annabel's carrier on the floor by the window and rushed over, still amazed that she *did* have a daughter. The baby girl was sleeping and looked so peaceful. She'd made an appointment with a pediatrician in town for Annabel, but from what she could tell, the infant looked healthy.

"Coffee?" Daisy said, picking up the pot. "I was just about to pour myself a mug. It's decaf, though."

"I'd love some."

Daisy poured and brought two mugs to the table and sat down. "You should have seen Noah with Annabel the past seven weeks. I knew Noah was capable of surprising me, but he *shocked* me. When I called my brothers to tell them, they didn't believe it and thought I was exaggerating."

Sara added cream and sugar and took a sip. "Exaggerating what?"

"His devotion to that baby. The note said she was his, and that was all he needed to know. He loved Annabel from the minute he brought her inside, I think. You know how many times he watched a YouTube video about burping a newborn, how to position the bottle while feeding? Like twenty times. I went with him to the baby emporium in Prairie City, and he spent ten minutes picking out a wipes warmer." She chuckled. "Noah Dawson walking around the ranch holding a baby in pink footie pajamas, introducing her to all the new animals. One time she fell asleep, and he shushed the goats."

Again Sara wanted to smile and cry. "Our Noah Dawson. I wonder what happened to him."

"I think the ranch did, Sara. He was the one of us who loved this place. He was the baby of the six of us and the Dawson kid who lived here his whole life. Our half brothers were whisked away by divorce and only came to visit. I don't think it's in their blood the way it is in Noah's. And the letter our dad left him, wanting him to reopen the guest ranch? Something got fired up in him. Purpose. Legacy. A future."

Sara nodded. She understood all that. What she would never understand was why she hadn't been that for Noah when they'd been together. Maybe she was flattering herself or being whiny, but their friendship ran so deep and so long, and their attraction, which he'd denied both of them for years, had been crazy intense. But he'd let it all go.

Eh. Didn't matter anymore. She wasn't here to revisit their past or figure out the mind of Noah Dawson. She was here to get her life back, get back on her feet, be her own woman again. She'd save up and then she'd be on her way with her children, starting fresh.

"Did you and Noah figure out what your role will be on the ranch?" Daisy asked. "I'd love for you to help me out with the guests. Our first group is coming on Friday afternoon and staying the week. There are twelve of them sharing the six cabins. Each cabin can accommodate more people, but the group leader wanted each attendee to have a lot of space, mental and physical."

"Ooh, the female empowerment group. Noah mentioned them."

Daisy nodded. "The leader is a life coach. I might linger in the back of the room to eavesdrop on the sessions."

"Me too. Female empowerment is exactly what I need right now."

"Ditto," Daisy said. "Big fat ditto."

Sara took a sip of her coffee. "I just realized that Noah and I didn't talk about *any* of the details of my employment at the ranch. Childcare issues and all that. He did say we'd work out the logistics before the staff meeting on Thursday, when he'd introduce me to everyone."

"I'm sure he intends to be your childcare provider," Daisy said. "And Mrs. Pickles is available. And me too whenever I can. I really do need the experience."

"I feel really lucky," Sara said, taking a sip of her coffee. "You Dawsons were always wonderful to me."

"You're like family," Daisy said, touching Sara's hand.

"You're going to make me cry." She blinked back being such an emotional hormonal mess, but she was too touched and her eyes welled. "Did Noah tell you about your dad leaving me the garden plot my mom built behind the foreman's cabin?"

"Another thing my brothers and I couldn't believe," Daisy said. "The thoughtfulness involved in that. Just when you think someone doesn't care about a damned thing, including himself and his kids, he stuns us all with handwritten letters."

"You liked the letter he left you?" she dared probe.

Daisy seemed lost in thought for a moment. "It touched me. And I really fought it. But yeah, it touched me. I'm not really ready to talk about it, though."

Sara nodded. "Totally understand."

The screen door opened and there was Noah, and the sight of him almost had Sara blushing. He was just so intensely sexy. Without remotely trying. He had that tall, lanky, muscular physique, the low-slung dark jeans and dusty boots, the brown Stetson. And that face that she'd loved since she was so young, the star of her nightly dreams and fantasies.

The man who'd taken care of a baby girl left on his porch in the middle of the night. Who'd watched videos on burping and shushed noisy goats so she could nap while he walked her around the barn.

That old stirring ignited deep inside her, and she tried to toss some cold water on it from the bitter part of her heart, but then Noah came over and knelt down in front of the carriers, touching a finger to Annabel's cheek and then Chance's.

"How are these little rabble-rousers?" he asked, his expression so tender.

I. Cannot. Like. You. That. Way, she told herself. *Cannot*.

Heaven help her.

Chapter Five

"Wait," Sara said, putting her suitcases beside the bed in Noah's guest room, which would now be her bedroom. "This is your office."

"Not anymore." Noah took the big empty box in his hand and filled it with the contents of the desk by the window, then took the bulletin board off the wall and tucked it under his arm. The room had never felt like an office, and though he stored paperwork here, he didn't like to sit at the desk. He preferred the kitchen table with a view of the barn and Bolt's head poking out of her corral, which also afforded a view of the main drive up from the gates. He also liked to work in a corner of the living room with a view of the wilderness and a winding trail that led up to the main house. "Now it's your room."

"I don't want to displace you," she said. "We can move the bed into the nursery. The babies don't need their own room, really."

"Yes, they do. Because as you know, taking care of a baby is exhausting and you need *your* own space, a door to close."

She shot him an appreciative smile. "How'd you get anything done when it was just you and Annabel here?"

"I took her with me everywhere. In the ole Snugli. If I couldn't, Daisy or Mrs. Pickles would watch her for me. The crew I hired did the heavy lifting when it came to renovating. I directed."

She grinned. "I can just see you, telling the crew what to do with a pink-outfitted baby strapped on your chest."

"Hey, two of them were dads themselves. They high-fived me every day about it."

She bit her lip and turned away.

Uh-oh. What had he said? "Sara?"

She dropped down on the bed. "Just waiting for the other shoe to drop, maybe. This all seems too easy, Noah. Things falling into place for me—first with reuniting with Annabel and having her safe and sound. Getting just the right job and place to live. You—my new boss, by the way—being this new person."

He got it. Her trust in everything had been shattered.

"You know what you need?" he asked.

She tilted her head. "What?"

"Some time to put your feet up and relax. Come down when you're hungry."

She raised an eyebrow, and he realized he was pushing it, being too much the host when she expected very little from him.

Which hurt, he also understood. He'd show her who he was.

Or not, actually. His entire focus could now be on the ranch. For the past seven weeks, he'd had no idea how he was going to get everything done for opening weekend, the most important weekend of his life, with a baby in tow. But he had. Thanks to a solid team, thanks to Daisy, thanks to him caring about both the baby and the ranch more than he'd ever cared about anything.

Except Sara. And he couldn't let his residual feelings for her, which he'd been trying to tamp down since she'd stormed the drive in that Range Rover, get him distracted. The Dawson Family Guest Ranch wasn't just about him; his siblings had invested in the place. They'd entrusted him with their money and their faith, and he would not let them down. Or himself.

Just about two months ago, Annabel had been added to that list. But now he had to take her off— somehow. She wasn't his baby, and Sara wasn't going to stay here forever.

The real problem was that he couldn't imagine ever crossing Annabel off the list. Granted, it had been only hours since he learned the truth that he wasn't the baby's father. But inside, he was. And always would be.

A cry, slightly different than Chance's, came from the nursery across the hall of the foreman's cabin. Annabel. Sara's heart leaped, and she bolted out of bed with a glance at the clock—1:14 a.m.

Her first middle-of-the-night wake-up from the baby girl she thought she'd lost. She'd never been so happy to be pulled out of bed in her entire life.

I'm coming, sweetheart, she thought as she hurried across the hall into the nursery. *Your mommy's coming and will never let anything happen to you again. Ever.*

She stopped in her tracks in the doorway. A half-naked Noah sat in the glider by the window, Annabel nestled in his arms, the moonlight a soft glow around them. He was so focused on the story he was telling the baby that he didn't even seem to realize Sara was there.

"And then Hermione ran and ran and ran," Noah said, "and poor Dylan—he's one of our cowboys— tried every trick to get the black-and-white goat to come back. The *main* trick is to actually let the goat chase you. Yup, just start running in the direction you want Goaty to go and wham—back in her corral."

"Is that what happened?" Sara interrupted with a smile as she stepped into the room.

Noah looked up at her, his gaze lingering a beat longer than it normally might and she realized she was wearing her skimpy pajamas—a Wyoming Wildcats T-shirt and a pair of yoga pants with a heavenly stretchy waistline. No bra, and motherhood had done wonders with typically B-cup breasts.

He cleared his throat and smiled at her. "Hermione is especially strong-willed. She wanted the high grass on the far side of the field by the fence, so Dylan had to wait until she was ready to play chase." He frowned suddenly and carefully stood up, glancing down at Annabel, whose eyes were drooping. "I'm so used to rushing in at her every cry. I should have let you take care of it. Sorry."

"It's nice that two people care so much about her, Noah," she said, then instantly regretted those words. Did she want Noah to care about Annabel the way she did? Of course, she understood why he did right now, but once a little time passed and he got used to not being Annabel's parent, the bond would loosen, right? Seven weeks certainly wasn't a lifetime.

A blip, he'd called it. She realized now, based on how he was looking down at Annabel—like a loving, doting father, something her daughter had not experienced for even a second from her biological father—that Noah had been lying. Seven weeks weren't a blip to him. He'd said that for her sake—and Annabel's. Because he truly loved that little girl.

"Do you think Willem had a moment's pause?" she asked, unable to stop herself. "Did he reach into the car to get her carrier when he arrived at your cabin in the middle of the night, the rain probably having started, and look at her face and think, *this is my daughter, my baby girl, my son's twin sister.* Did he ever think that for one second?" A sob tore out of her throat, and tears threatened.

Bloody hormones.

She watched Noah gently lay Annabel in the crib beside her brother, then he walked over and pulled her into his arms and held tight. She let herself sag against him—again, his strength, the comfort he was offering everything she needed right now.

"I want to hope so, Sara. I think we should just leave it at that."

She nodded against his chest. His bare chest. Warm, hard muscle, soft skin.

Stop needing this so much, she told herself, unable to pull away. But in the difficult past weeks, the past few months, the past couple of years, allowing her husband to isolate her from friends to the point that she hadn't felt comfortable turning to anyone even after losing her baby daughter, she *did* need this embrace.

Noah didn't pull away either. "C'mere," he said, and led her by the hand out of the room and into her own.

He stopped in front of her bed and held up the pretty blue-and-white quilt, embroidered with little stars and crescent moons. Part of her frowned. The other part tingled. She could barely take her eyes off his chest, and when she did, his face was even better. The beautiful face she'd loved and dreamed about for so long, full of tenderness, his blue eyes blazing with what might even be desire.

But come on. "Um, I guess it's been the requisite six weeks doctors tell you to wait after childbirth, but it's only a week past." Why had she said that? It wasn't as if she'd let herself go there with Noah anyway.

He raised an eyebrow. "Sara. Get your mind out of the gutter," he said with a grin. "I'm putting you to bed—alone. Get your rest."

Oh. She felt her cheeks burning a little. *Embarrassing!* Maybe Noah wasn't attracted to her anymore anyway. *You are being jerked around by hormones*, she reminded herself. *Ignore yourself. Just go back to sleep like Noah suggested.*

She slid into bed, laying her head on the soft down pillow. He actually tucked her in and then leaned over and kissed her forehead. Oh God, now she might cry. Her dad used to do that. And she always felt so loved, so protected, so safe in the world.

"Sleep, Sara," he said, straightening. "If you hear a baby crying, just turn over. I've got it. I won't expect to see you until at least 9:30 a.m. That way we can talk over your role at the ranch before the ten o'clock staff meeting. It'll be a good time to introduce you to everyone."

She couldn't even speak. She was just too overwhelmed. By her thoughts, by him, by her life right now. She nodded and then tried to find her voice. "Noah," she finally said as he neared the door.

He turned around.

"Thank you for everything."

"My pleasure," he said with such sincerity in his voice that her eyes did well up.

Danged hormones.

It *was* the hormones, right?

Brilliant sunshine streamed through the woven shades on the window, and Sara had no idea what time it was. Given how well rested she felt, how ready to bounce out of bed, it had to be past eight o'clock. When was the last time she'd slept in?

She grabbed her phone from the bedside table: 8:17 a.m. Heaven. She'd woken naturally, not from a crying baby or an alarm clock, though hers would have gone off at eight thirty.

The twins hadn't woken her because Noah had obviously taken care of the early-morning waking; she had no doubt they were either napping in the nursery or that he was downstairs with them right now, chatting away with them about ranch life or telling a story about the goats or sheep. Noah had gone from being someone she'd run away from to a man she trusted with the lives of her babies, including the baby girl she'd just been reunited with.

Still, part of her, a big part, felt uneasy about that. Putting her trust in anyone was a bad idea. Noah Dawson was going to be her boss. Their relationship was something different now. Another new normal she'd have to get used to.

After a quick shower, she dressed in white leggings and a floral tunic, which she hoped would be appropriate enough for the staff meeting, dried her hair and then headed into the nursery. The twins were asleep. Heart at ease and filled, she tiptoed out. If they were taking their morning naps, Noah had also gotten up with them at around five and fed them and changed them and taken care of them. He'd been up with them last night as she had, and he had to be exhausted right now. Today was likely to be a very busy day for him—tomorrow was the grand reopening of the Dawson Family Guest Ranch.

She headed downstairs, also appreciating the smell of coffee. Noah was sitting at the round table by the window, a clipboard with what appeared to be a checklist, various folders, his phone, a mug of coffee—and a baby monitor, of course, in front of him.

He was in jeans, a dark green Henley shirt and barefoot. Sexy feet.

"Sleep well?" he asked, taking a sip of his coffee. His gorgeous blue eyes were sparkling with energy. Or maybe just adrenaline. If the man was tired, he didn't show it. She realized he was on new-parent time—used to the crazy hours of caring for a newborn. His schedule and hers had been exact the past several weeks—an hour's distance from each other. There was no way he wasn't tired, but he made it work because he had to.

"I think I actually got almost seven hours, thanks to you. A new record."

"Good. You needed it. I can't even imagine what all that shock yesterday did to your system. You needed a solid night's sleep."

Huh. She hadn't even thought about that aspect. "I appreciate that."

He nodded. "So how about we talk about your job on the ranch, then we'll have the staff meeting, and then I can take you on a tour of the place, since it's changed from when we grew up here."

"Sounds good." She poured herself a mug of coffee, added cream and sugar, and sat down beside him.

"So, I figure you can either be the assistant foreman, as you were on the Circle D with your dad, or you can take on a specific position—I could use an education manager and workshops leader to run the information sessions and classes we'll offer about ranch life and the petting zoo. Or you can be a cowgirl and lead rides and teach the basics. Or a housekeeper, though Daisy already hired two. She also hired a receptionist who'll have the welcome-slash-check-in shed as her station by the gate, but we could use another. Cowboy Joe could always use another pair of hands in the kitchen. In terms of splitting the running of Dawson's, as I mentioned, I'm land and animals and maintenance and all that falls under that, and Daisy's guests, lodging, food and all that falls under that. As assistant foreman, you'd be both our right hands. It's a big job but one in your veins. And it pays well." He told her the salary, noting all employees would also receive holiday bonuses since the staff would have to work on most holidays, taking shifts so they could still spend time with family.

"Assistant fore*woman*, it is," she said, extending her hand.

She liked the idea of taking a job she knew and understood. She'd worked alongside her father for years as a teenager at Dawson's back in the day, and she'd been the assistant foreman—forewoman, in her mind—at the Circle D for years afterward, a position she'd loved. When her dad had gotten too sick to keep working, she'd switched to part-time to take care of him.

Willem had once told her that he liked that she smelled like goat when they were dating, because it made him feel like she wasn't a gold digger. Of course, she had married him for his money and he knew it; she'd never lie to herself that she'd loved him, though she had liked and appreciated him before she'd known who he truly was. It was how she'd not seen the real Willem back then that worried her. Maybe the truth was that she'd ignored what she'd needed to because what he'd promised had been more important than his snobbery and disdain of perfectly normal things.

Maybe she was doing something of that herself now. Ignoring her past with Noah because what she needed from him was more important right now. A job with room and board in a place that she loved, that felt comforting and familiar, where she felt on solid ground when she was anything but.

Just be smart, she reminded herself. *Build your trust in yourself and your judgment. You're in the right place for yourself and the twins for the right reasons.*

"Sara?"

She blinked and realized Noah was holding up his coffee mug in the air as if to clink in celebration over the job. She was glad to be pulled out of her thoughts. She held up her mug, and they gently clinked and took sips.

"Welcome back to the Dawson Family Guest Ranch," he said. "Assistant Forewoman."

His smile lit up his handsome face, and she was pulled back into seeing the old Noah—the one she'd been so in love with she could hardly look at him sometimes. How she'd loved that face, dreamed about it.

Noah was now her boss. Not the old love of her life. Not an ex. Her boss.

She'd keep her attention on that word, and she'd be okay. She now had a great job, was living in her old home, one where her father had never been sick or weak, one where her mother had still been alive for the first nine years of Sara's life. She had her mom's garden plot to revive. By summer's end, she might even have enough saved to start her new life, though now that she thought about it, she wouldn't have two built-in sitters-slash-bosses like Noah and Daisy. Things *were* going to be good here.

Maybe too good to leave, though. Which doubly meant she'd have to keep her distance from the way Noah made her feel. Safe. Everything felt so fragile, so tentative, so new, and there was no way she could count her chickens or think anything was squared away. Things could change in a heartbeat. People could turn. You just never knew.

Just earn your money, build your bank account and take care of your children, she reminded herself. That was her purpose. To be self-sufficient and never rely on anyone again.

"You remember Mrs. Pickles, right?" he asked her.

"Of course," she said, the image of a middle-aged woman with a long red braid and bright green wellies coming to mind. "The babysitter. Daisy mentioned she's helped out a few times." What she couldn't remember was Mrs. Pickles's real name; her surname had been long, so she'd told everyone to call her Mrs. Pickles, and it had stuck as she'd watched over Noah and Sara until Daisy was considered old enough to keep an eye on them and a couple of the ranch hands' kids too back when.

"She's been a godsend. I hope you don't mind that I called her and told her we could use her services for a few hours of wake time and a few of nap time for the twins going forward, and then I realized I had to tell her a bit of the story. She said she'd love to work for us. She has twin grandchildren herself, high schoolers now, so lots of experience."

"Perfect. I noticed their nap times seem in sync. Both were still sleeping when I checked on them a little while ago."

He nodded. "Annabel always woke from her morning nap around ten, so I'm thinking one of us can be home to do wake-up, feeding, a little playing, then hand over to Mrs. Pickles. She can watch them for three hours till the next nap, then stay for that three-hour stretch, so it gives us a good six-hour workday uninterrupted. Then, either one of us will be with them or we'll take them in the ole Snugli on the job when it's appropriate."

No wonder she trusted him with the twins. He was completely on top of everything—from ranch details to their schedules.

"They should sleep right through the staff meeting if Daisy and I keep it to no more than twenty minutes," he said. "It's really for everyone to meet one another. When the twins wake up, I figure we can put each in a Snugli and I'll give you the grand tour."

She liked that he wanted to take the twins with them, not just cast them off to a sitter the whole day. He truly wanted to be with the twins and to immerse them in the ranch life, because it was his life. *Their* life.

Once again she found herself overwhelmed at how thoughtful he was, how kind. She felt very lucky and wanted to wrap her arms around him in thanks.

She really had to force herself not to.

Chapter Six

"I'm real happy for you two," Cowboy Joe said after the staff meeting as everyone headed to their respective stations to make sure everything was in place for tomorrow. He stood in front of Noah and Sara, each with a baby strapped on their chest, outside the main house. "I remember you both running around the ranch as kids, getting into mischief. Now you're a family raising the next generation of Dawsons to carry on the legacy of this beautiful place."

Noah stared at the tall, skinny man—the ranch's cook—in the brown Stetson and shaggy gray beard, wondering what on earth he was talking about. Then he realized Cowboy Joe thought he and Sara were a couple—and the parents of the twins. Some of the staff had met Annabel when they'd come for interviews if he'd been unable to secure his sister or Mrs. Pickles, and of course he'd introduced her as his daughter. So when he'd introduced Sara as Annabel and Chance's mother, those who'd met Annabel naturally figured he was the dad and that there was a twin brother who they hadn't met before.

Hey, fine with him. He'd always feel like Annabel's dad, and he was glad to put Chance in the mix too. Plus, Cowboy Joe's presumption had not only given him a second shot with Sara, but a lifetime in the family sense. He liked that too. The *idea*, actually. Because romance was the furthest thing from his mind. Romance took over, kept you up nights, and he was already up nights—bleary-eyed but *clear*. He didn't need his brain and newfound structure and vision and purpose turned upside down over what his heart was doing. He'd never let himself mess things up with Sara again, anyway. Too much was at stake for that.

And he was flattering himself if he thought she'd ever give him a second shot.

"Come by the caf later to test out my new blueberry muffin recipe," Cowboy Joe said, giving each baby a gentle tap on the nose. "I'm planning on them for the welcome baskets Daisy asked me to make up for the group coming tomorrow," he added over his shoulder as he headed down the path.

"Will do," Noah called after him.

"So everyone thinks we're a couple and that you're the twins' father?" Sara asked.

"Probably."

She was quiet for a few seconds, staring off into the distance. "I guess the real story is a little too complicated."

"Way too complicated." He upped his chin toward the path. "C'mon. I'll show you the main barn."

As they walked in the brilliant late May sunshine, a perfect seventy-three degrees, which would hold steady for the entire week as some kind of cosmic gift, he pointed out the different kinds of trees and birds to Chance in the carrier on his chest.

"See that beautiful black-and-white quarter horse, Chance?" he asked, pointing straight ahead where Bea, one of the ranch's cowgirls, was grooming the horse in front of the big red barn. "His name is Batman. He's getting all spiffy for the big day tomorrow. One day, you'll ride him, Annabel beside you on Bolt."

Sara went quiet again. Until she said, "You should know… I'm not really sure what my future holds. I don't know how long we'll be here."

Sharp right hook to the kidney. "What?" he said, also feeling like a hay bale had just fallen on his head. "You just got here. I just hired you. You haven't even had your first day of work yet. Suddenly you're leaving?"

He looked at Annabel—well, the back of her, anyway—strapped in the carrier on Sara's chest. *That's my baby girl. She's not going anywhere. She belongs here.*

Dammit, dammit, dammit. He knew the truth of who Annabel's parents were. Why wasn't it helping?

"I didn't say that, Noah. I only said I didn't know how long we'd be here. By the time these two are old enough to get on a horse? I don't know."

He stared at her for a moment, not liking the direction this conversation had taken one bit. "Well, I don't know why we're even talking about that, then."

"I just want to be honest and open," she said, a hand protectively on the side of the carrier. "I know you're attached to Annabel. So…"

Attached to Annabel. Attached? Was that all she thought it was?

"So I think we should continue with the tour," he said, a little grumblier than he probably should have.

"Fine," she said.

"Fine."

To have something to do, they both started walking over to where Bea stood with Batman.

"Hi," Bea said, putting down the grooming brush. "I finally get to meet this little charmer up close." She bent toward Chance in the carrier on Noah's chest. "Aren't you precious. Just like your twin sis. I'll name the outdoor petting zoo enclosure for you so you'll each have your own special honor."

"Special honor?" Noah repeated.

"Go see," Bea said, gesturing at the petting zoo a quarter mile up from the main barn. The gleaming yellow barn with its white trim had several enclosed pastures for the animals, the goats and sheep grazing. Their two alpacas were in their own large area, as were the six ponies. "I wanted it to be a surprise for opening day," she added with a big smile. "I checked in with Daisy a couple days ago—she said you'd love it."

Oh hell. A couple of days go, everything was very different than it was today. A couple of days ago, he was someone's father. Now he wasn't. "Well, thanks in advance," he said, knowing Bea's heart was in the right place. "That was sweet of you, whatever it is."

He glanced at Sara, who smiled at Bea, and then they headed up the path to the yellow barn. Inside, the top half doors open to bring in the light and fresh air, the floors freshly swept and the pens recently cleaned, his attention immediately fell on a large sign handwritten in colored chalk on the wall of the barn: the Annabel Dawson Petting Zoo Barn. The sign listed rules of the barn. Not to feed the animals inside the barn. Not to enter the corrals. To wash hands before leaving. That was listed three times to stress its importance.

He glanced at Sara. She was staring at the sign, her expression...tense.

Annabel Dawson.

"Bea didn't know," he said quickly. "Nor did Daisy a couple days ago when Bea checked in with her. It's just chalk. It's easy to erase Dawson and write in Mayhew. Or we can just erase the whole thing."

Since you won't be here long anyway.

She reached a hand to Annabel's head in the sea-foam-green cotton cap, her shoulders slumping. "I keep forgetting how hard this must be for you," she said, turning to face him. "She's been your daughter for almost two months. A Dawson like the sign says. Now here I come, erasing her last name on her specially named barn. Talking about leaving one day." She stared down at the ground.

Right? he wanted to say. Smugly. Honestly.

Ragingly.

Until he thought about what *she'd* been through the past two months.

His phone pinged with a text, and he was grateful for the interruption, because what the hell was there to say about all this? The truth was what it was, and Sara had been through hell. Potentially losing Annabel to her rightful parent—and distance—was nothing compared to what Sara had had to deal with, what she could have believed her whole life.

He pulled out his phone. The text was from Carly, the receptionist and gate greeter.

Four guys who look like you just drove up and are heading toward the welcome shed at the gate.

What? Four guys who looked like him sounded like his brothers, but there was no way they'd be at the gate.

Yup, I called it, Carly added. They said they're your brothers, here to see you.

Whoa.

He pocketed his phone in what felt like slow motion, his brain not quite catching up. "I can't believe I'm actually about to say this, but my brothers are here."

"Wow," Sara said, her expression brightening. "Didn't you say they all refused to step foot back here?"

He nodded. "Wonders never cease." That rolled

off his tongue, but nothing was truer in his life right now than that old adage.

"You go meet them, Noah. I'll take myself on the tour. I know my way around, even if things have changed."

Things had changed, but not the basic paths, and Sara knew those walkways and trails, including the ones that led into the woods, with her eyes closed. Plus, he had no doubt she needed a little space right now. From him.

"I'll just need to get the double stroller from the cabin."

"No need to walk back there. See that shed?" he asked, pointing out the half door. "I keep a lot of different supplies in there, including for Annabel. There's an infant stroller. I can put Chance in and you can take him on the tour with Annabel in the Snugli."

"Is there anything you don't think of?" she remarked.

He glanced at her, catching the surprise in her eyes, her tone.

"Not anymore. It's my business to think of everything."

She half smiled and they headed over to the shed, where he took out the stroller, diaper bag attached.

"You really do have this parenthood thing down," she said, staring into the diaper bag. "Pacifier, wipes, a changing mat, diapers. A bottle, bottled water and a small container of formula."

"I worked at it." *Harder than I ever worked at anything, even rebuilding the ranch.*

She held his gaze for a moment, and he couldn't read her expression, so he took Chance out of the front pack and put him in the stroller, not a peep out of him. He unstrapped the Snugli and folded it in the stroller's basket.

"If you need me," he said, "just text or call, and I'll be wherever you are in a heartbeat."

She held his gaze again, and he still couldn't read her. She nodded. "Go see your brothers. We'll be fine."

As he watched her continue up the path toward the guest cabins and the creek beyond, he couldn't move. And suddenly it didn't just feel like Annabel was moving away from him with every step, but all three of them.

His phone pinged again—Carly at the welcome shed. They said they'd meet you at the farmhouse.

He turned and headed in the other direction, forcing himself not to turn around to watch Sara and the twins get farther away.

Focus on your brothers, he told himself. Hadn't Ford said hell would freeze over before he'd come back to the ranch? Hadn't Rex said he was done with the place to the point that it bugged him to think about Noah getting it back up and running?

They were here, and that was all that mattered.

Same with Sara and the twins.

As Ford—who as oldest still declared himself in charge of the grill—put the perfectly cooked steaks on a platter, Noah glanced around at his four brothers and sister sitting around the patio table in the backyard, unable to believe the Dawson guys were really here. They'd spent the first half hour making small talk and catching up a bit, then Ford had gotten busy cooking. Apparently, the siblings had planned the surprise visit to the ranch a week ago, so they'd shopped in town for a pre–opening night celebratory dinner involving New York strips, baked potatoes, asparagus and craft beer.

Surprise didn't begin to describe how Noah felt. Shock was more like it.

But here they all really were. Ford. Axel. Rex. Zeke. And Daisy, who he was used to seeing, of course, but he certainly didn't take her being here for granted. When he'd first arrived at the farmhouse and seen his five siblings in the yard, he'd gotten all emotional and had to take a moment. Now, they were yakking like they saw each other all the time; it was always like that when they finally did get together.

MELISSA SENATE 131

Despite having three mothers among them, the siblings looked a lot like. They had varying shades of brown hair, some very dark like Axel's and some almost blondish like Daisy's, and they all had their father's clear blue eyes. The six of them were tall, including his sister, who was five foot nine. Everyone always said it was lucky she got the tall gene too because standing up to five brothers, four of whom were older, was easier when she at least reached their chins.

Ford was from their dad's first marriage, which apparently had lasted two months before his mother found Bo Dawson cheating not once or even twice but three times and finally left, then discovered she was pregnant, dropping off little Ford every other weekend for years. Axel, Rex and Zeke were from the second marriage to one of the other women who'd left hard-living Bo for the reliable, friendly mail carrier, whom Bo had tried to beat up but had been too drunk and ended up punching himself out. Axel, Rex and Zeke had all been too young and small to carry him inside, so they covered him with a few sleeping bags and put a bag of frozen peas on his purple-and-black eye and let him sleep it off.

Noah and Daisy were from Bo's third attempt at marriage, which lasted until their mother died in a car accident when Noah was nine. *He's trouble,*

but he's my trouble, their mom would say, thinking she had the smarts, sense, work ethic and financial savvy to manage both their lives and their
children's, so she could be with the man she loved,
despite his flaws. She'd been kind to the four older
kids too when they'd come for their visitation. Daisy
had once told Noah she thought their mom was romantic *and* half-crazy, that she'd never be so reckless
with herself. Anyway, after their mother's death, Bo
had gotten a vasectomy, and word among the women
who hung out in the sticky-floored bars he liked to
frequent was that he carried around a letter from his
doctor confirming he'd had the procedure so that no
one could pin a pregnancy on him. A good-looking
man, tall and lanky with an easy smile and flirta-
tious manner, he still managed to bring home lots of
women, who never stuck around long. The Dawson
name still carried weight in those days.

"I thought you said something about hell freezing
over," Noah said to Ford as they all got busy digging
into the plates and bowls on the table, thanks to Ford,
who'd nixed their offers of help with dinner. Ford had
always been the Dawson who could do anything and
everything—from cooking to wrangling troublemak-
ers—he was a police officer out in Casper.

"Well, it kind of did," Ford said. "Daisy let us
know that not only were all renovations on sched-

ule and according to plan, but that the place looked even better than it did when Gram and Gramps ran it. And that you pulled it off with a baby strapped to your chest the past two months. Tipping my hat to you, Noah."

The praise felt good. "Well, a little determination and all your help, and the Dawson Family Guest Ranch is back."

"Our help?" Axel repeated, heaping butter on his baked potato. "What did we do, Noah? You did it on your own." A search and rescue worker, Axel had always had big expectations for the word *help*. He spent his days and nights rescuing the lost and injured from area mountains. His most recent mission—involving a toddler whom he'd eventually found and reunited with his mother—had almost done him in.

"Um, he had our *financial* help," Rex pointed out with a grin. What Rex did for a living to have helped so much in that department was anyone's guess. He clearly had money and liked nice things, so he did *something*, but he'd always been cagey about it. Noah and Daisy used to joke that he was a CIA agent. For all they knew, he could be.

"And Daisy was here," Noah added, twisting the cap off his beer. "I had her help too."

Daisy raised her sparkling water. "Sometimes I

think about how if you hadn't found a baby on your porch, I might still be in Cheyenne."

"Speaking of daddies," Ford said, eyeing Daisy. "You ever going to tell us who the father is?"

She frowned just slightly, and Noah could see how conflicted she was about the guy. "The two of us are talking again. We weren't when I first found out I was pregnant. So let me see how things go, and then maybe I'll introduce him. Maybe I won't ever get the opportunity. We'll see."

"Sounds complicated," Rex said. "You need to sic your brothers on him, you say the word."

Daisy's eyed widened, then she grinned. "Why do you think he's still anonymous?"

There was some reminiscing about the times they did face down any guy who'd dared mess with their little sister. Even Noah, two years younger, but closer to Daisy than any of the Dawsons, had been protective of her.

"Well, speaking of *babies*," Zeke said, turning to Noah, "when do we get to meet our little niece? Who's watching her right now?" Zeke, second oldest, was the businessman of the bunch, a corporate cowboy who wore suits with boots and was never without a black Stetson; in fact, he wore one right now. Noah had been in touch with Zeke the most of all his siblings besides Daisy, since every month he sent Zeke his ranch ledgers, and every month Zeke sent back a satisfying: *I'm impressed. You know what you're doing on all levels, kid bro.*

Noah took a swig of his beer. "That's kind of complicated too."

"Which part?" Ford asked in his cop tone.

"After dinner, you'll hear the whole story," he said, glancing around at all of them. "And meet Annabel."

He was about to add *and her twin brother*, but that would pause forks and beer bottles and require immediate explanation. As he'd walked up to the house to meet his brothers just an hour and a half ago, he'd texted Sara to ask how she wanted to handle said explanation, and she said she'd like to come over for dessert, twins in tow, and tell the story on her own terms.

There were some raised eyebrows and shrugs and everyone resumed eating. Daisy sent him an encouraging nod. For the next fifteen minutes they talked about the guest ranch's bookings; Noah had a solid lineup of guests coming all summer and into fall, and Zeke said he had no doubt word of mouth would fill out the empty cabins along the way. All the brothers agreed the place looked great, that the more modern aesthetic—rustic-luxe spa meets dude ranch—would appeal to a wider range of people, and it had. Noah had stormed the offices of every small and big newspaper in the county—the daily and the free weeklies—with press releases Zeke had helped him write from afar and photos as soon as prime spots were camera ready, like the cabins. The Dawson Family Guest Ranch 2.0 had gotten solid press, and the phones started ringing with bookings. People remembered the place—many locals and those spread around the state had spent their family vacations at the ranch, so that had also worked in its favor.

"Well, let's eat up so we can meet Annabel and hear this complicated story," Ford said, eyeing Noah. Again, cop face. Nothing got by Ford Dawson. Noah knew his older brother had long felt responsible for his younger siblings, living with them only part-time growing up, and now at a distance of hours.

Luckily Noah had already finished his steak and a heap of the roasted asparagus in garlic butter, his favorite vegetable. Because his appetite was shot.

"Hey, is that Sara Mayhew?" Rex asked as he and Ford came out the sliding glass doors to the back patio with three kinds of pie for dessert.

Noah turned and shielded his eyes from the glare of the sun, just beginning to make its descent. Sara was coming up the path from the foreman's cabin, wheeling the double stroller. She wore a long black sundress and sandals, a straw hat on her head, her silky brown hair in a braid down one shoulder. She looked like a vision and he could barely take his eyes off her.

"Sara *Perry*, right?" Zeke corrected. "I occasionally saw photos of her and Willem Perry in the society pages of the *Converse County Gazette*. Once I ran into them at a fund-raiser and hugged Sara hello, and Willem practically grabbed her away from me. I'm surprised he didn't take a swing at me." He tilted his head. "I read he died in a car accident a couple months ago. Is Sara okay?"

Noah glanced around at the shocked expressions, barely hearing the murmurings of "how awful" and "he was so young" and "poor Sara." None of them knew Willem the way he and Sara did—Sara most of all, of course—because the three of them had been the same age, had come up in school together. "She'll *be* okay," Noah said, offering her a smile as she got closer.

As Sara arrived on the patio, the group got up to say hello and offer condolences. She handled that well with brief thank-yous and nods, accepted their hugs, and then conversation thankfully turned to oohs and ahhs about the babies.

And then, from Ford, his focus on the twins: "So

who's who? I assume one is Noah's daughter and one is yours, Sara?"

"Actually, they're both mine," Sara said, adjusting the sun shade on the stroller so the Dawsons could get a better look. "Annabel and Chance are twins."

"Wait," Axel said. "Daisy told us Noah found Annabel abandoned on his porch in the middle of the night—right before a major rainstorm." As a search-and-rescue specialist, those details would be foremost in his mind. "Since I'd have a hard time believing *you* left your daughter like that, there has to be a story here."

Four sets of blue eyes turned to Sara, then Noah. Daisy already knew the details, of course, but even she was staring at Noah.

"There is," Noah says. "And it's ugly. I'll let Sara tell it," he said, sitting down. The brothers took his solemn cue and all sat back down at the table.

"Why do I think we're going to need whiskey for this?" Rex asked, leaning back and crossing his arms over his chest.

"It's as ugly as Noah says," Sara began and then launched into the story.

The expressions on his brothers' faces said it all.

"Wish I could arrest the bastard," Ford said, shaking his head. "I've seen a lot in my time on the force, but this?" Disgust was palpable on his face. "Have you spoken to police about the midwife's actions?"

"Not yet," Sara said. "Willem's lawyer did a little digging for me after we found out what Willem—and she—had done. She officially retired the next day."

"How are you planning on handling that?" Ford asked.

"I'd like to pay the midwife a visit," Sara said. "I know there's no excuse for what she did, given her job, her responsibility to her patient and the baby she was hired to help deliver. But I also know that Willem threatened her and that he had something on her. I'll plan on seeing her in the next couple weeks. I've just got a lot to focus on right now."

"If you need help or an escort for the visit, you let me know," Ford said.

"I will. And thank you."

"You know what I can't stop thinking about?" Daisy said. "How lucky it was that Noah actually heard Annabel's cries at two in the morning outside his window. He's always been a light sleeper. A herd of buffalo couldn't wake me up."

"Oh, trust me, one tiny peep out of your little one and you'll be bolting up," Sara assured her. "Mother radar is strong stuff."

Daisy smiled. "Glad to hear that." She took a sip of her seltzer. "You know, given what your late husband did, Sara, things sure worked out all right. Noah *did* wake up. He saw the note saying she was his and took immediate responsibility—he even had her checked out by Doc Bakerton at 2:30 a.m. And then just seven weeks later, the truth is revealed in that letter. Willem's whole terrible plan was interrupted within two months. Someone up there was sure looking out for you."

"I think about how it could have been decades," Sara said, shaking her head.

"Cosmic justice," Axel said. "Sorry if I'm speaking ill of the dead, but…"

No one disagreed. That the plan had been foiled so early because Willem had been killed in an accident and had left that "last laugh" letter for Sara did seem like cosmic justice.

Noah loved Annabel with everything in him, but now that he knew the truth of her parentage and her brief history, he wasn't Team Ignorance Is Bliss. It wasn't—and never was. Annabel deserved to know her mother; Sara deserved to be with her daughter. Things had worked out for the best for the two of them. Except when it came to what Noah would have to give up when Sara—as she put it—left one day.

"The twins are beautiful, Sara," Axel said, standing up and peering in the stroller.

"And look just like you," Ford noted.

"Didn't Noah say that Annabel looked just like him?" Rex asked with a grin. He peered closer at the baby girl. "Uh, maybe the coloring—hair and eyes. But that nose, that chin, the shape of the eyes, even her expression—all Sara."

Humph. Noah really had thought Annabel looked something like him; he had from the moment he'd brought her inside. Yeah, she'd looked more familiar than like him, but *still*.

"And both twins are safe and sound," Zeke added with a nod.

They all raised their bottles to that.

"Well, hell," Axel said. "I say they're our *honorary* niece and nephew."

As everyone clinked to that, Noah noted that Sara's smile was genuine.

So what did that make him? Honorary dad?

As the group crowded around the stroller to take closer looks and photos of their honorary niece and nephew, Ford held back.

"You okay?" his brother whispered.

"Somehow," Noah said. More glumly than he meant to.

"Probably because you care more about Sara than you do about yourself," Ford whispered back. "Always have, right?"

Noah sucked in a breath. He was always surprised

at how well his siblings knew him when they didn't get together very often the past ten years. But suddenly he understood why Ford, who'd led the intervention in Noah getting his act together *and* rallying the siblings in support of Noah's determination to rebuild the Dawson Family Guest Ranch, believed in his youngest brother. Because Ford *did* know him. And that confidence in him meant the world to Noah.

Yes. He did care more about Sara than about himself. Always had, always would. Except for those months two years ago when he'd finally given in to his attraction to her, despite how bad he knew he was for her, when he'd been at rock bottom without realizing it, putting on a good show with the small ranch he'd bought until he couldn't hide who he was back then: his father's son.

As Ford joined the others in fussing over the twins, Noah couldn't take his eyes off Sara, who'd never looked more beautiful, Annabel in her arms.

Everything that meant anything to him was in this backyard, on this property right now, including the ranch itself. And the best way to take care of Sara and the twins was to make sure the ranch was a big success. Annabel and Chance would always have a home here, Noah's own grandparents' home for many years. There was family history here for them, and he wanted Dawson's to succeed for them.

He owed his siblings that too—for their investment in the ranch and in him. He couldn't fail,
couldn't lose sight of the prize: steady bookings,
good reviews, word of mouth. Nothing could get
between him and making this ranch everything it
needed to be for his family—and Sara's.

*So keep your distance from her, no matter how
attracted you are to her.*

Not going to be easy, since they were not only
sharing a cabin, but essentially a workplace. He was
her boss, and he was going to have to keep things
very professional between them.

And his thoughts were anything but professional
as he took in how beautiful she was, how sexy, memories of their brief romance hitting him left and right.

*If you care about her, you'll keep your hands and
lips to yourself.*

He made that silent vow, then headed over to
where the group stood around Sara and the babies,
his head clear, his heart guarded.

Chapter Seven

After a brief tour of the guest ranch and more hat tipping to Noah at what he'd done with the place, the Dawson brothers—except for Ford—got back in their rented truck and headed off to the Airbnb they'd booked in town. There were free rooms in the main house and a bunch of comfortable couches in the lodge, but between being honest about the place still having too many bad memories attached *and* not wanting to distract from the big day tomorrow, Axel, Rex and Zeke opted to stay elsewhere. Sara had gotten the impression that Noah understood; he still seemed to be marveling over the fact that they'd come at all. Ford had been cryptic about why he wanted to stay at the house, and Noah hadn't pushed, but Sara sure was curious. Ford was the Dawson sibling who held the worst memories of the ranch.

Now, just after 9:30 p.m., she and Noah were in the nursery, putting the twins to sleep in their crib. She stood beside Noah as he told a story about Batman, an Appaloosa, escaping his stall and running all over the ranch in search of the perfect carrot. Noah's voice was so soothing, so beautifully familiar, that even Sara almost fell asleep, but the twins were out within two minutes.

"My work here is done," he said with a smile, but it quickly faded.

"Everything okay?" She knew he had a lot going on, a lot on his mind, but she had a feeling he was still thinking about their conversation in the barn earlier that day.

"Are you planning to leave?" he asked, finally turning his head to look at her. "If you are, I want to know. I need to prepare myself so I'm not blindsided by losing Annabel."

She liked how direct this new Noah was. But then again, this wasn't a conversation she could have now. How could she possibly answer him?

"I have no idea what I'm doing, Noah. Right now,

I want to be here. I *need* to be here. That's all I know."

He crossed his arms over his chest. "So maybe you'll stay for a couple of months."

"I really don't know. I guess it depends on how things between us are. And right now, they're not good."

He stared at her. "In general or this minute?"

She felt herself relaxing. "This minute. And the minute earlier in the barn."

"I don't want to run you out of here," he said, taking her hand. "I want you to stay."

If she wasn't mistaken, he'd been about to add the word *forever* but then clamped his mouth shut.

So why did that make her feel so…prickly? Because that *want* had nothing to do with her and everything to do with his love for the baby he'd thought was his daughter?

Maybe. That should make absolute sense to her. It wasn't as if she wanted Noah Dawson to be romantically interested in her. Did she?

Oh hell. She did a little. Because she was still reeling from all that had happened and needed a pair of strong, familiar arms? Or because her residual feelings for him would never, ever fade? Noah was her first love. Her only love. Yeah, she'd been married. She'd also had some short-term relationships over the years that hadn't gone anywhere—maybe because she'd never felt about anyone the way she'd felt about Noah. Despite how wild he'd been, how she hadn't been able to tame him. He'd done that reining in himself, now that she thought about it. Maybe that was why she was even remotely thinking about him *that* way.

When she was ready to find love again—though that felt very far off—she'd look for a man who'd be a great father to her twins. Like Noah.

She'd look for a man who was responsible and reliable in ways she could plainly see. Like Noah.

She'd look for a man who sent little chills of anticipation up her spine at the thought of kissing him, of being in bed with him. Like Noah.

Oh hell. She was sunk!

She wanted to flee the room *and* fling herself into his arms. That's how much she couldn't get a handle on herself.

She needed fresh air and more open space, somewhere his tall, muscular, sexy being couldn't dominate. She gave his hand a squeeze. "Let's go enjoy the gorgeous night. We can sit outside and *not* talk."

He laughed. "Let's do that."

Downstairs, he grabbed a baby monitor from the hallway console table and they headed out to the front porch, so big and welcoming. His sister had told her she'd planted all the beautiful flower boxes that hung from the windows, and there were four white rocking chairs and a porch swing along the side porch where it wrapped around. They opted for the swing, Noah giving them a push with his foot.

She had the urge to wrap her arm around him, and whether she should or not, she was going to. Doing so earned her a smile and Noah scooting a bit closer. "How many nights did we sit here and look at the stars and not talk because there was too much to say and we both knew what the other thought anyway?"

"I feel like that's both the case and not, now, though," he said. "We do have a lot to talk about, but it's so complicated—and not—that there's really nothing to say at all." He shook his head. "Did any of that make sense? Was it actually English? Between you saying things like you're leaving and my brothers' surprise visit, I'm a little out of whack."

"What if I promise I'll stay the summer at the very least?" she said, turning to look at him.

He got up abruptly and walked to the porch railing, facing away from her, then turned around. "Great. So three more months of getting attached to Annabel and now her brother and then you'll leave? That's great, Sara."

"I thought we weren't going to talk because it's too complicated."

"I don't push things under the ole rug anymore," he said. "You talk or you fester and implode. I'd rather talk."

"I suggested the summer because you'll know we're staying put for at least that long."

"I *love* Annabel, Sara," he said, a fierce edge in his voice. "She's my daughter. There, I said it. She's my daughter," he shouted into the sky. "I know she's yours, but she's mine too."

Sara gasped. "I get it. I do."

"Marry me. Let's get married. That's the solution. Annabel stays forever. And not only that, but I get to be dad to her twin brother too. The twins grow up in the place where they have so much family history. Both Annabel and Chance will have a loving, devoted father. You'll have the security of the ranch that means home to you. And to sweeten that end of it, I'll split my share of the ranch with you fifty-fifty. You'll be an owner, with the same share as I have."

She gasped again. It was all too much to take in. The marriage proposal. The security. The ranch ownership.

The marriage proposal.

All because he felt like Annabel's father in his heart, in his blood and veins and every cell in his body.

Security—for the twins and for herself when she

was penniless with maybe $1,100 in jewelry to sell if she needed to.

Home—when the Dawson Family Guest Ranch was home and always had been.

And if the place went belly up, if Noah reverted to his old ways and ran the place into the ground?

He won't, a voice inside her knew full well. *He cares too much now. His family is involved. Annabel is involved. And now you and Chance are added to the mix.*

And you believe in him.

"I need some time to think," she said, turning away. It was all too much.

"Am I being selfish here, Sara?" he asked, stepping closer. "I know what you went through with Willem. Why you said yes. Am I asking the same thing of you?" He took a step back, regret all over his face. "You know what, forget I even brought up the word *marriage*. After everything you've been through, it's not fair to you."

She studied him—hard—and his sincerity was clear. His sincerity had never been the issue. "I don't think you're being selfish. I understand where you're coming from. You're making me an offer, Noah. What Willem did, what I accepted, was very different. Or it *feels* different, anyway. But I do need time to think."

He nodded. "Take all the time you want. I'll go

do my rounds on the animals. Need anything before I go?"

A hug. A bear-hug.

She shook her head. "I'll just sit out here awhile
and then probably go up to bed."

He nodded. And then she watched as the man
who'd just proposed to her headed down the path
toward the red barn.

Marry Noah Dawson? Once, that had been her
dream. Now it might be her only option for security
for herself and the twins. But more, she understood
Noah's depth of love for the baby he'd rescued, had
thought was his, had raised, even if it was for barely
two months. How could she take Annabel from him
when the baby meant so much to him that he was
willing to give up his freedom for her?

Maybe that was what put a check mark in the
no column. When she'd dreamed of marrying Noah
Dawson, love was the biggest factor. Now, it wasn't
even on their radar.

Noah moved sideways through the stables, giving
each of the thirty-two horses a pat and a little pep
talk for tomorrow. He was expecting twelve guests,
which meant twelve horses would christen the new
and improved Dawson Family Guest Ranch's trails
and fields. And though Noah would do his best to

match rider to horse based on the guest's level of experience or lack thereof, sometimes, they'd have to see how it went. Which meant having lots of solid, sweet, well-rested horses to choose from. "Based on the initial questionnaire the guests filled out," he said to horse twenty-seven, Blaze, "you'll definitely be paired with our most experienced rider. Do me proud tomorrow." He gave Blaze a pat.

He'd gotten up to horse number thirty, Sugar Cube, when he finally broke, when he couldn't pretend to have only the ranch at the forefront of his mind.

"I proposed, Sugar Cube," he said to the silvery-white quarter horse with the soulful brown eyes. "Proposed marriage. What if she says no? What if she says yes?"

Sugar Cube didn't respond, but she still got her pat. Noah moved to the next stall, Goldie, and told the gorgeous palomino with her gold-colored body and white mane that he had no idea what Sara's response was going to be. "Think she'll say yes? She might? Then we'll both have what we want and need. Right?"

He'd still considered Sara his best friend the past two years when they hadn't spoken or laid eyes on each other, when they'd known nothing about each other's lives. That was how strong their connection was. To him, anyway. That seemed like a solid basis for marriage. Much more so than the hot and cold of fleeting love with all its passion and arguments. Best friendship: lasting. Real. He'd let passion intrude on that friendship two and a half years ago, and what happened? He'd run Sara off into the arms of a psycho.

He'd be able to raise Annabel and Chance. They'd be his children for real. And his precious Sara, whom he cared about to the moon and back, would be beside him, sharing his life, his world.

"It wasn't impulsive," he told Bluebell in the next stall, giving her a pat. "I mean, it was. I didn't think of it until that moment, but it's probably the smartest thing that's come out of my mouth ever." He reached the end of the stalls, patted King and felt the tension leave his shoulders.

As he was leaving the stables to head back toward the main barn, he noticed his brother Ford walking about a hundred feet ahead, just around the side of the pasture fence. Ford was staring at a piece of white paper, then looking down, then around. He had something in his other hand. Looked like a narrow pitchfork.

What the hell was he doing?

"Ford?" Noah called out.

His brother jerked his head up, clearly surprised. "Just looking around."

"Sure you are," Noah said, walking over to him. He glanced at the piece of paper in his hands, which looked like some kind of crudely drawn map. "What's that?"

Ford sighed. "My legacy from Dad."

"Ah." He suddenly realized why Ford "Hell Will Freeze Over Before I Step Foot on the Ranch" Dawson had decided to stay the night at the main house.

"A map of some kind?" Noah asked.

Ford nodded. "It was folded up in the letter he left me. The letter rambled on about how one night when he was drunk and angry at my mother over an argument, he put her diary, which he'd jammed open with a knife, in a metal box and buried it somewhere near the stables. Or he thought near the stables."

"Her diary?" Noah repeated. "You sure you want to find that?"

Ford sighed hard. "Apparently my mother had a secret. That Dad knew about. He wrote that my mother flew into a rage and tore up the property looking for the diary but never found it. Then I guess she gave up on it, figuring he was too much of a drunk to ever dig it up himself and use it against her, since he'd likely never find it."

"Any idea what the secret is?" Noah asked.

He shrugged. "Who the hell knows. I'm not sure I want to know. But Dad's letter said it's something I *should* know, that he's sorry he wasn't a better father to me or any of his kids. I figured while I was here tonight, I might as well try to find it, since Dad made a point of saying it was far off any of the trails or paths. I didn't want to do anything to mess up the grounds the night before opening day. I've just been poking into the dirt, hoping to hit on something hard."

"I'll help," Noah said.

For a minute there, Noah thought lone-ranger Ford was going to say, *nah, you've got a big day tomorrow, I've got this*, but Ford replied, "I'd appreciate that."

Noah jogged over to the stables and got a sharp-ended tool, then jogged back over to where Ford was poking the ground in circles. "Let me see the map."

Ford handed it to him. "This seems to be the area," Noah said, taking in where his dad had drawn the stables with a few horse heads poking out, the tree line, the five-hundred-plus-acre pasture. There was an X on a tree trunk—a tree that seemed to stand alone. And the only tree that stood alone was close to where Ford was poking with the pitchfork.

They poked and poked and poked, walking in circles and squares, but both came up empty.

"I had a feeling I wouldn't find it," Ford said. He shrugged. "Just thought I'd give it a try."

Noah glanced around at the grass. There was just too much land to cover. "I can keep looking when I get the chance. And you can always come back."

Ford ran a hand through his hair. "I might. We'll

see. Sometimes it's better not to know." He shook his head. "I'm not sure I mean that. I don't know."

Noah got the sense his life wasn't the only complicated one.

"I'll be heading out first thing," Ford said. "Good luck tomorrow. I know this place will be a big success."

Noah extended his hand, and Ford glanced at it, then pulled his youngest sibling into an embrace.

"You did good, Noah," Ford said. "With the ranch, with Annabel. With whatever's going on with Sara and both twins, considering that they're all here."

Noah nodded, Ford's words of praise a boosting balm as he embraced his oldest brother. "I'm trying. Hard." *To the point that I* proposed.

Let her say yes when I get back to the cabin, he thought.

Sara sat in the kitchen, on her third cup of decaf, picking at the leftover peach pie that Daisy had packed up after dinner for Noah to take to the cabin. She heard the key in the lock, and her pulse leaped.

Yes, no, maybe so. She had no answer yet. Her answer was all of the above.

Noah came into the kitchen and gave her such a forced casual smile that she laughed. Sara could plainly see how tightly wound he was right now and how he was trying to fight it.

Because he'd proposed and wished he hadn't? Because he worried she'd say no?

She took a sip of her coffee. "I'll get right to the point. If we're going to put a marriage on the table, we'd better square away some important details."

She could see the relief in his eyes, the way his shoulders relaxed some.

He got himself a bottle of water, then sat down. "At least it's up for discussion."

She was about to blurt out, *Well, I did it once before with a monster, so why not with my one true love?*

Which just made her feel worse, more tied up in knots over the whole damned thing.

"Noah, marriage is supposed to be sacred. It's supposed to mean something more than a mutually beneficial partnership."

"That's what it is for everyone who gets married," he said. "A couple is madly in love. That's mutually beneficial, so they marry."

She raised an eyebrow. "You know what I mean."

"I do. And my point still stands. We've got a lot of water under the bridge, Sara. And we have some very good reasons to band together and do this. Unless you think your soul mate is out there, waiting for you to be ready. Do you?"

She stared into her coffee for a moment, his words jabbing her in her chest. "You obviously don't think either of ours is. Or you wouldn't be proposing what's basically an arranged marriage."

He took a swig of his water. "I guess different things are more important to me now. I figure to you too."

She stood up and walked to the window, looking out at the night, at the pasture, at the Wyoming wilderness beyond. "What the hell happened?" she asked.

She could see in the reflection from the window that he stood up.

"What do you mean?" he asked, concern deepening his voice.

She turned around. "This entire conversation. A marriage of convenience. How the hell did my life come to this?" She stalked over to the chair and sat down. "I'm just whining and feeling sorry for myself. I'm pissed, Noah."

He sat back down too. "You have every right to be angry. But that isn't my aim—to dredge up bad feelings. If that's what the proposal is doing to you, let's forget it. You stay here as long as you want. I just want you to be happy and feel safe."

She glanced at him, her eyes welling. *I just want you to be happy and feel safe.* A person who said that was a person who cared about her. And he was the only person saying anything like that. Her family was gone. Her friends scattered. She had no one left.

"I used to believe in soul mates," she said. *You, you big dope. You were my soul mate.* "I don't believe in that stuff anymore, Noah."

He leaned forward. "Let's be each other's family, Sara. You, me and the twins. A family, right here where it all began for both of us in so many ways. And you'll have half my ownership of the ranch."

Could this work? If she didn't believe in love and romance anymore, if her first marriage had blown everything she'd once cared about to bits, then why not accept a partnership with Noah Dawson? They'd set terms. They'd treat each other respectfully. They'd get what they needed.

"I'd never take any part of your share of the ranch, Noah. But yes," she added, standing up again. "I will marry you."

Before Noah could stop himself, he got up and held out his arms, and Sara rushed into them. He could feel her holding herself a bit stiffly, which he completely understood. This hug was about gratitude on both sides, about the friendship that would never fade, no matter what. It was their handshake on an agreement.

"I was so afraid you'd say no, Sara." He found himself holding her an extra beat too long, inhaling the balsamy scent of her hair, remembering how good having her so close against him used to feel.

She stepped back and leaned against the counter. "We should discuss logistics, of course."

He nodded and sat back down.

She did too. "Let's just go to the town hall. There's no waiting period in Wyoming. We could be married in the morning."

"My head might explode," he said. "Getting married right before the ranch reopens. How about we wait till the first group leaves? That'll give us time to decide if we're telling people about this or keeping it our secret. If we're wearing rings." He took a drink of his water.

"But there are some issues we can settle right now," she said, looking everywhere but at him.

"Like?" he asked.

"Separate bedrooms. No sex. No kissing, no touching, no hanky-panky of any kind, Noah Dawson. We're making a deal for those mutually beneficial reasons you listed. I don't want any confusion about what the marriage is."

He wasn't so sure they had to make any proclamations. Who knew how things would evolve?

Then again, sex had destroyed their relationship once and sent her away.

On one hand, he could see them returning from a

long day, a problem with a guest, a sick calf, and having the urge to take her in his arms and kiss her, hold her, this beautiful woman he'd loved for so long and who'd share so much of his life going forward. He'd always been so physically drawn to Sara, including right now. How would he tamp down these feelings?

He'd just have to. Because on that other hand, the confusion she'd mentioned had the potential power to ruin their arrangement entirely and send her away again. He couldn't risk that.

He took in one last long drink of her luscious body, her pink lips, her brown eyes and long silky brown hair. He closed his eyes for a half second, vowing that when he opened them, he'd see her as discussed: off-limits.

"Agreed," he said. "We're friends. We won't let anything get in the way of that and what we're doing."

She gave him something of a smile that didn't last very long. "Good. Then we have a deal."

The problem was that the vow he'd just made to see her as off-limits wasn't working. She was still sexy as hell. But if there was one thing Noah Dawson had developed the past few months, it was self-control.

He'd do this because he *had* to.

Chapter Eight

The next morning, at just after 11:00 a.m., Sara stood beside Noah and Daisy outside the Dawson Family Guest Ranch lodge as a silver van pulled up in the parking area. The first guests had arrived, and she could feel the Dawsons practically vibrating with excitement and nerves.

The weather couldn't have been better—blue skies, brilliant sunshine, low humidity and sweet breezes in midseventies temperatures. Sara smoothed her hunter green polo shirt with the ranch's logo on the pocket, Staff spelled out in caps on the back. Last night, Noah had knocked on her door and said he'd forgotten to give her an employee shirt; all staff would wear the green shirts and jeans during working hours.

When he'd held up the shirt in her doorway, she'd been so moved by it, by her memories, that she'd wanted to pull him into her bedroom and never let him go. She'd had a Dawson's staff T-shirt when she was a teenager. She still had it, though she was a size small back then and seven weeks after giving birth, Sara was a definite L for large. The old one was a burnt tan color, and she liked the forest green even better. The new shirt reminded her of all good things, of new beginnings. Before Noah had knocked on her door, she'd wondered how she'd sleep with questions of their pending marriage looming in her thoughts. But somehow the green shirt representing her employment, money coming in, *security*, had her falling asleep within a half hour.

The twins had woken her up twice, and a third time, very early this morning, she'd gone into the nursery to find Noah already taking care of business. He'd looked wide-awake and alert, excited about his first guests. Mrs. Pickles was with the twins now in the cabin, and Sara liked that she just might see the sitter wheeling them around the grounds in the stroller during the day.

A thirtysomething redhead stepped off the van,

shook hands with Noah and Daisy, and then Noah introduced her to Sara as Connie Freedman, the life coach running the retreat.

As the retreat participants came off the van— eleven aside from the coach—Connie introduced everyone. But Sara was surprised—and thrilled—to already know one of the women, an old friend from high school named Tabitha Corey. Since the retreat was getting underway immediately, Sara would have to wait to catch up with Tabitha until this evening.

As guest relations manager, Daisy led the group to their cabins to settle in before the tour, opening session and meet and greet of the horses Noah had chosen for each participant. But Sara couldn't help but notice most of the guests looked kind of…glum.

"Is it my imagination, or do the guests not look very excited to be here?" Noah whispered.

"Oh wait," Sara said. "The retreat is called Get Your Groove Back."

"What does that mean—exactly?" he asked, tilting his head. "I thought it was about getting some R and R."

"Well, that too, but getting your groove back generally means you've lost that spark and you want to find it. A recharge kind of thing for the heart, mind and soul."

Noah raised an eyebrow. "I just ride Bolt when I need that."

She smiled. "That's why they're here. Nature helps. Horses help. Inspiring talks help. Like-minded people who won't make you feel like you're whining or just need to man up or chin up. Hopefully they'll look very different in a week."

He nodded. "I'm pretty sure I recognized one of the guests—and her name too. Tabitha Corey. We went to high school together, right?"

Sara nodded. Tabitha looked very in need of a recharge, even if she was in full Western regalia, the kind of outfit that said she'd gone all out on new riding gear and Stetsons and Western-style shirts when plain old jeans and T-shirts would do. Sara couldn't help but be curious about why Tabitha had signed on for the retreat. She had been a golden girl, the kind you couldn't hate because she was kind and friendly to everyone, even if she was a queen bee. She'd recently gotten engaged to a tall, good-looking endodontist Willem had played squash with, but they hadn't socialized as couples. Willem would insist on showing up for fund-raisers and important events, but then he'd want to leave after fifteen minutes, which had always been fine with Sara. She'd noticed the diamond ring on Tabitha's finger. Huge. And she looked like a million bucks, despite the lack of light in her eyes. Sara couldn't help but wonder why Tabitha was here.

As the afternoon went on, Sara helped both Daisy and Noah in various capacities, and she found herself loving the fast pace and constantly changing duties. This morning, before the guests had arrived, she'd double-checked the cabins with Daisy to make sure they were all ready with welcome baskets and fresh wildflowers and had all the necessary supplies. She'd helped Noah and Dylan in the main barn with lining up the saddles the guests would likely be using. Since the group would hit the cafeteria for lunch at twelve thirty, she'd stopped in a bit before to see if Cowboy Joe needed any help. He had everything under control with his small staff. Lunch was his specialty, chili and corn bread, and the entire caf smelled amazing.

At two, the life coach and retreat director, Connie, was giving a talk called "What Happened to My Groove, Anyway?" in the lodge. Sara had been assigned to work the concessions counter, offering coffee and tea and lemon-infused water and snacks, and she'd been riveted by Connie within a minute. The life coach was in her late thirties with pretty shoulder-length red hair and dark brown eyes, in a forest green pantsuit that managed to look woodsy and professional at the same time. Connie stood at a podium in front of the eleven seated participants, who all held little silver notebooks. Sara had never met a life coach before, but Connie's talent at public speaking and conveying her message was an immediate given.

"Feeling stuck," Connie was saying. "Knowing you're stuck and knowing there are probably steps you could take to get yourself unstuck but being too down in the dumps to do anything but mope on your sofa with a stack of tabloid magazines and the remote control and a family-size bag of sour cream and onion potato chips. And a two-liter bottle of soda. And a big bag of fun-size chocolates." She gazed at the group. "How many of you can relate?"

Sara's hand shot up in the air before she could stop herself. She pulled her hand down, but not before Connie sent her an encouraging smile. Twelve hands, including Connie's, were up. Sara wanted to stick hers back up too. Hell yeah, she could relate.

"But guess what?" Connie said. "All of you, every single one of you, has already started the process of getting yourselves unstuck, getting your groove back. Because you're here. You did something proactive. You got off the sofa, figuratively and literally." She smiled. "Round of applause, ladies." Connie clapped, and so did everyone else, including Sara, down low under the table.

Maybe she shouldn't be cheering herself on, though.

She hadn't gotten herself off the sofa—figuratively speaking. She'd been propelled off it by Willem's death. She'd learned the truth about her daughter, sped over to the ranch and here she was. In a new life entirely.

But she had to wonder just how long she would have lived under Willem Perry's thumb. Being chastised for installing the toilet paper roll the "wrong" way. Night after night, unable to dislodge the lump in her chest, in her throat.

"We all have our breaking points," Connie continued. "You're all here because you're either close or you've reached it and you're ready to break out, break free, be who you actually are."

The part about the breaking point made Sara feel better; she'd reached it—she'd briefly left during her pregnancy and had been pulled back out of fear, but she would have figured out a way to leave again. She was sure of that. And anyway, going over this was pointless. She was in a new life—with her son and daughter. What mattered was what she did with her present and how she planned for her future—their future.

She frowned as she recalled how sure she'd felt earlier about accepting Noah's proposal. But had she been operating out of fear, out of feeling like she was stuck? She had a job, a place to live, a good roof over her babies' heads. She was earning her way here. Noah had offered her half his share of the ranch to sweeten the security deal, but she didn't want that from him. She'd never take that from him.

Suddenly she was only 50 percent on the idea of marrying.

There was a solid week between now and when they'd go to the town hall to legally become husband and wife. She'd see how things felt.

"Sometimes, the hardest part can be doing just that—getting up, asking for help, making a commitment to yourself," Connie went on. "And sometimes the hardest part might be yet to come—really examining what you want and how to achieve that. Sometimes we don't feel like we deserve what we want, let alone to actually get it. I'm here to tell you, we all do deserve it. So at this retreat, let's commit to giving ourselves a chance. Baby steps, big steps, whatever you're ready for. We're all on our way!"

Yeah! Sara almost cheered as she straightened the bananas in the pretty blue bowl on the table.

Connie handed out schedules and outlined the rest of the day—next up was being matched with horses, so the group got up, a few stopping at the concession table for the lemon-infused water or a coffee or a piece of fruit. As the participants left the lodge, former golden girl Tabitha hung back, then came over to the table and made herself a cup of coffee. She looked amazing—gorgeous long blond hair, light makeup that looked completely natural, the fancy Western outfit and dark pink cowboy boots. But she sure didn't look happy. Newly engaged to a young Brad Pitt endodontist or not. And, of course, she was here at a retreat for getting her groove back. Sara would have never in a million years thought Tabitha Corey had ever or would ever *lose* her groove.

You never know what goes on in someone's private life, Sara thought as Tabitha stirred her coffee. *Appearances are deceiving. Yup, I know all about that.*

"So far, so good," Tabitha said, a hopeful light suddenly in her pretty hazel eyes. "Right?" But then the light disappeared and she seemed so conflicted. Something was definitely bothering her.

Sara reached out a hand and covered Tabitha's. "I'm not even a participant in the retreat and I feel empowered." She smiled.

Tabitha nodded and seemed about to say something, then she lifted up her coffee cup as if toasting in agreement and shuffled out, catching up with the rest of the group.

Sara wanted to run after her, give her a hug, tell her she was here for her if Tabitha wanted to talk, but she could see Connie now standing next to Tabitha, chatting away as the group headed to the barn. She had a good feeling about Connie and what this week would give all these women. Maybe even Sara herself.

Her phone pinged with a text. Daisy.

Have fifteen minutes to help set up the meditation room in the lodge? Second floor event room.

Meditation? Sara thought. *I might lie down and stay there myself.*

Be right there, she texted back.

Between the retreat and her job, Sara just might get her own groove back. If she watched her step with Noah Dawson. And she would.

The barn hadn't collapsed. A horse with a guest on its back hadn't gone rogue, throwing her fifty feet in the air. No one had gotten food poisoning from Cowboy Joe's chili (not that they would). These and many more were the irrational fears that had kept Noah up at night when he should be getting any chance of sleep he could, particularly with two babies in the cabin. But opening day of the Dawson Family Guest Ranch had gone off without a hitch so far—knock on every piece of wood in the vicinity.

He stood at the small barn beside his cabin and gave Bolt, whom he'd just returned to his stall, a piece of carrot. Then he lifted his face to the gorgeous late-May sunshine and breathed in the warm, breezy, fresh air. Between the weather and the total lack of problems, he could almost relax, but he'd save that for the end of the week. He'd spent the past hour with the retreat guests in the barn and pasture, first making sure they were matched to the right horses for their level and comfort and then joining in on their first ride in the huge expanse of prairie to the right of the main barn. Satisfied that the group was comfortable and set for the time being, he'd left them in the horse leader's capable hands with Dylan and Bea, the ranch hands, who'd ride alongside the group as backup.

About to walk the paths to keep a general eye on things, Noah saw Mrs. Pickles come out of his cabin with the twins in their double stroller, using the ramp he'd built. That tiny burst of joy, still so unexpected, went kaboom in his chest at the sight of the babies.

"There are my sweet twins," Noah said, walking over with a smile. He leaned over and unbuckled Chance, carefully lifting him out of his infant seat.

He froze, just for a moment, sucking in a breath. *My twins?*

Reaching for Chance as easily as he would Annabel?

The little cowboy had worked his way into Noah's heart just as his sister had. And just as fast. He couldn't really even think of Annabel without thinking of Chance; they were a pair, a package, a set. Individuals, but he loved them with equal ferocity.

Oh God. He did love them. Both. Hard.

"I was hoping to run into you, Mrs. Pickles." Sara's voice came from down the path. There was tension in that voice, if he wasn't mistaken.

He turned around, Chance cradled against his chest. Sara was coming from the direction of the lodge. As it had earlier, the sight of her in her Dawson Family Guest Ranch staff shirt shot straight to his heart, and despite his vow to keep his mind off how attracted to her he was, every cell in his body went on red alert. "Same here. And I did."

She smiled sort of vaguely, her gaze on the baby in his arms. What? Why did she seem uneasy?

She leaned over the stroller and gave Annabel a kiss on the head, then got as close to Chance as she could while keeping her body as far away from Noah as possible, and deposited a kiss on her son's head.

Hmm. She was definitely bothered by something.

"These two are such good babies," Mrs. Pickles said, grinning at her charges. "I love watching them. And what a lovely day for a walk."

"Well," Noah said, putting Chance back and running a finger down Annabel's cheek. "I won't keep you." He turned to Sara. "I was about to take a walk of my own on a grounds check. Join me?"

"Sure," she said. She leaned over the stroller. "'Bye,

sweets," she cooed to her twins. "See you later. I love you," she whispered.

Then they both watched as Mrs. Pickles wheeled the stroller toward the lodge.

"There goes my heart," Sara said, her expression wistful as she stared after the sitter and the stroller.

He stared after them too, then looked at Sara. "I know what you mean."

She frowned, took one last look at the retreating figure of Mrs. Pickles, then turned for the path toward the main barn.

So he was not mistaken that something was bugging her. And it was something *he* was doing.

"You seemed uneasy before, when you saw me holding Chance," he said, walking beside her.

She turned and looked at him. "I hate that you know me so well, Noah Dawson."

He grinned. "Actually, us knowing each other so well might make things easier. Because it makes us talk about even uncomfortable stuff."

"I also hate talking about uncomfortable stuff." She bit her lip. "I guess I'm just taking everything in, Noah. The idea of getting married. What that will mean going forward. About the twins too."

He stopped. "What do you mean?"

"You already feel like Annabel's father," she said. "You're going to feel like Chance's father too."

He was already beginning to.

She crossed her arms over her chest. "And I'll have to factor you in when I think about what's right for me and the twins. How did that happen? When did you become a vital part of my plans for my life?" She frowned and turned away.

"When—"

She whirled back around. "Rhetorical question. I know, I know. When you brought Annabel inside and took responsibility for her. When a note said she was yours."

Damned right. But he understood how strange that must be for her. And yeah, maybe even unsettling. He wasn't Annabel's father. He'd met Chance the day Sara arrived on the ranch. Noah shouldn't factor into Sara's decisions for herself.

But he also couldn't help how he felt or that circumstances had unfolded as they had. Her baby girl *had* been left on his porch. He *had* taken her in. He *had* claimed responsibility. And he *loved* Annabel. She'd always feel like his child. Chance now did too, because he was Annabel's brother, because they were living in his cabin, and the little guy had grabbed hold of his heart and wasn't letting go.

"Ah," she said with an exasperated tinge to her voice and throwing her hands up in the air. "I get your side. I get my side. But I need to get *my* groove back, Noah. Sounds cute and all on retreat flyers, but it's serious stuff and hard work, and I don't know that coming into my own means marrying you for security." She shook her head. "In fact, it doesn't."

Oh hell. He understood that too well. He'd had to fight his butt off to stand up again—and the only person he'd been fighting was himself. He'd found his way. He wasn't going to stand in Sara's while she worked out her past.

"If you're telling me you've changed your mind about getting married, I...understand," he said, holding her gaze for a moment, and then he had to look away and let the disappointment sock him in the gut. She'd leave. She'd leave and take the twins. Not immediately, not even in a few months, but a new year always meant something to Sara, stood for new beginnings and possibilities. She'd probably leave by then.

"That would kill you, wouldn't it?" she asked. "If I told you I changed my mind. I think that's what bothers me, Noah. That it would."

"Should I be honest? It would. And you know why."

"Yes, because of Annabel," she said.

"And Chance. They're a pair."

Tears welled in her eyes, and he took a mental step back. He was overwhelming her, and that wasn't fair. She knew he meant it—that he loved Chance too. And that was killing *her*.

He put his hands on her shoulders. "Look, Sara. I want to be very clear. I like the idea of getting married and what that means for me as the twins' acting father. If you change your mind, yes, it'll knock me to my knees, but I'm all about getting up again. That's who I am now."

She stared at him. Almost looking confused.

He removed his hands and stuffed them in his pockets. "But I'll tell you something else. Yes, I have my good reasons for wanting this marriage, wanting you to stay with me forever. There are reasons involved that have nothing to do with the twins."

She tilted her head. "Like what?"

"Like that you've been my best friend since I was a little kid. Separated for the last two years or not. You mean a lot to me."

She gave a slow nod. "Same," she whispered.

He let that sink in for a moment, and it gave him the courage to say what had been building inside him the past couple of days. "And because—" He shut up fast. He couldn't say *that*. He took off his Stetson and ran a hand through this hair, glad he hadn't blurted out the rest of that whopper.

"And because what?" she asked, staring at him.

He had no idea why he thought she'd let him off the hook.

Hell. Just be honest. Say what's on your mind. "And because maybe, somewhere in there, months, years from now, whatever feels right—if it does—" Man, he was rambling. "Maybe there's a possibility of a second chance."

There, he said it.

He caught the intake of breath, the shielded surprise in her eyes.

But should he have said it? If he meant it—and he did—then why not? Why not put his cards on the table, say what he meant and felt? Even if it did get him knocked to his knees. Ignorance was never bliss. Everyone knew that.

His phone buzzed with a text.

"You should take that," she said fast. "I'll go check the main barn." She walked away—even faster—before he could say anything else.

A conversation we'll finish later. Or not.

He grabbed his phone. Carly, the welcome manager.

There's a reporter here from the Converse County Gazette. He says he's interested in writing a story about the grand opening. Should I let him through?

Noah's stomach flipped. Then flopped. A reporter. Press for the ranch: good thing. Bad press: bad thing. What if the reporter didn't like the looks of the place? What if something went wrong just as the reporter happened to be there, taking pictures and notes? An accident on the trail. An unhappy guest complaining about the water pressure, which was actually just fine.

You put your heart and soul into the reopening, he reminded himself. *Hired a top-notch crew. Everything is set for today. Everything is going great. The article will be glowing.*

Maybe. Or maybe not.

Cripes.

Why the hell was everything in his life so up in the air?

By the main barn, he could just make out Sara giving a wave to Mrs. Pickles, who was over by the small barn, pointing out the goats to the twins. *I have to believe in this place—for Sara, Annabel and Chance. If I don't believe in what I've rebuilt here, no one will.*

Noah's Magic Eight Ball answer had to come from himself: *It is decidedly so.*

Sure, send him up to the lodge, Noah texted back to Carly.

This was make or break for the guest ranch. Just like Sara marrying him was make or break for his heart.

Chapter Nine

Avoiding Noah in a twelve-hundred-square-foot cabin wasn't easy. Once Sara was officially off-duty, she'd rushed back to the cabin to take over from Mrs. Pickles and was there when the twins woke up from their nap. Over the next few hours, she told them all about opening day, her surprise at finding herself wishing she could sit in on every retreat lecture, and the even bigger surprise of running into Tabitha Corey. And then she started talking about Noah, how he'd rebuilt the ranch, how proud she was of him and how she couldn't figure out what to do.

Should I marry him?

Make a pro and con list, she could hear her mother saying any time she couldn't decide what to do about something, when both sides of the issue had check marks. She'd have to make it a mental one since she certainly didn't want to accidentally leave a piece of paper around with all that info for Noah to come across.

She sat on the sofa, Annabel finishing her bottle, Chance half-asleep in the swing on the floor beside her. *Okay, here we go, guys*, she told the twins.

Pro: I've known him forever. He will always feel like family, no matter what. I don't want to trust him, but dammit, he's given me no reason not to this time around. His sincerity leaps off him. I know the twins are safe with him. I do like the idea of them having a father—a father who actually loves them and cares about them and wants what's best for them, not himself. The sight of Noah Dawson gives me goose bumps. Everywhere.

Was that also a con? It was, given that the marriage Noah had proposed was like a business arrangement of sorts. Well, as businesslike as it got when children were involved. Scratch that, there was nothing businesslike about sharing a home and raising children together. This would be very personal. And Noah had said he liked the idea of a second chance—down the road.

Perhaps another con. How could she keep her

heart out of things in that case? When Noah did give her goose bumps?

Another pro: she adored his family. Daisy was right here. The ranch would be Sara's home on a permanent basis, and she did love this place. Everywhere she turned today, memories filled her. Her mother teaching her how to ride a two-wheeler. Her dad teaching her everything he knew about horses, his great love. Noah showing her a few secret trails he'd made that led to the river, where they'd fill backpacks with chips and the occasional stolen bottles of beer from both their houses, Sara hoping against hope he'd make his move, despite what he'd said. He never did. Not once. He'd written himself off as a jerk and told her she deserved the world. He'd seemed to believe that about himself to the point that it was automatic for him not to touch her.

She hated remembering that. And she'd hated remembering that he'd turned out to be right. Not about being a jerk; he wasn't. But about being wrong for her, unable to pull himself up and out of the hole he'd fallen into.

Pro: all these memories. Con: all these memories.

She sighed, cuddling Annabel against her and peeking over at Chance, who was just lying peacefully in the swing, gently swaying, fighting sleep as his little eyes drooped.

"Noah loves you both," she said to Annabel as she tilted up the bottle. "I really see that. If he acted like only you mattered, Annabelly, I could have reason to make some sort of fuss. But of course, he adores Chance too."

Every time she felt that frisson of fear about Noah getting too involved—as if there was anything more involved than the two of them marrying—she'd think about how he truly did seem to love both babies, and she'd feel that rush of gratitude that the twins were loved by someone else in this world. Someone pretty special, at that. She had no family, and Willem, an only child, had lost both his parents during the past five years. Noah really was the closest thing to family that she had.

Just when she thought she was acting out of devotion to the twins, making decisions for their sake, she'd feel that tap on her shoulder with the flip side, the other hand, the "yeah, but."

So am I marrying him or not? she silently asked both twins. *Am I committing to life with him as my best friend and my twins' acting father? Or am I committing to myself and finding my own way without needing security from anyone else?*

She heard his key in the lock, and on cue, goose bumps ran up her spine and along her arms and the nape of her neck.

"How are the twins?" he asked as he came into the living room.

She kissed Annabel's sweet-smelling head. "Fed, burped and ready for their cribs."

"Would you like to do the honors or should I?" he asked.

"It's kind of amazing that after hours and hours of work and running around, you're up for putting them to bed." *Because he's committed to them. Because he loves them.* "How about we both do the honors?" she said, getting up.

He smiled and took Chance out of his swing. The little guy fell asleep in Noah's arms before they even hit the stairs.

With both babies in their cribs, the lullaby player on a low setting and the door ajar, they headed back downstairs to the living room. Because Noah was Noah and would probably go into the kitchen to whip them up a three-course meal when he had to be exhausted, she beat him to it.

"I'm going to make us dinner," she said. "You sit and put your feet up."

"Dying to," he said, dropping on the sofa and putting his legs up on the coffee table beside the baby monitor. "Ah, that does feel good."

"Pasta with prosciutto and peas in a creamy pink sauce and garlic bread coming right up." She still had cravings for rich comfort food and had been dreaming of that very dish all day yesterday. A quick trip to the market last night, and she had the missing ingredients.

"Hurry," he said. "Now that you said it, I want it immediately. Five minutes ago."

She grinned and got to work in the kitchen, enjoying the domesticity.

Ah, another pro, she thought as she put the water on to boil and grabbed the prosciutto from the refrigerator and a cutting board from the cabinet. She liked cooking for herself and Noah because she liked Noah. Cooking for Willem had been a chore because he'd been so picky and finicky. Once, early on in their marriage, she'd grabbed his plate away when he'd complained how his steak looked before he'd even tried it and told him to make dinner himself, then stalked off. His passive-aggressive behavior that followed for days had ended up shaping more of her behavior and response to him than she'd realized. Willem had a been a gaslighter, making her feel crazy for complaining, and in her eyes, he controlled whether her father lived or died. So she'd kept the peace. And destroyed herself in the process.

Not exactly good companion thoughts for making a nice dinner. She poured herself a glass of lemonade and drank half, letting it refresh her, then set her thoughts on her twins and the hot guy on the sofa with his feet up.

Her head set back on straight, she sautéed the prosciutto and garlic, the delicious aroma taking over and making her stomach grumble.

"Can I help with anything?" Noah called from the living room.

Another for the pro column. "I've got it, but thanks," she called back.

How many times had she stood in this very spot at the stove, beside her mother or her father, and shared cooking duties with them? Her dad's specialty was his favorite dish, chicken parmigiana with a side of very saucy spaghetti. Her mom loved making every kind of seafood and salads with vegetables from her little garden.

There were times, particularly lately, when she thought about her parents and felt so sad that she'd need to sit down and just cry. But right now, sweet memories were coming at her, making her smile. Her parents had loved each other so much.

Con: marrying a man who doesn't love you that way.

Addendum: she used to believe that Noah *did* love her that way, even when they were teenagers, and that he truly was protecting her from himself. She'd believed he loved her during their brief and disastrous relationship two years ago. It was now that she wasn't too sure about. Noah was such a different person these days, and sometimes she couldn't even read him when she'd been easily able to before. His focus was brand-new to her, and it wasn't on her or a good time or sex. He was all about the success of the ranch—and now the twins.

But with that little hint of possibility he hadn't meant to utter aloud, *Maybe a second chance for us*...

Marrying Noah Dawson would be a leap of faith. Plain and simple. Who knew what would happen?

Con: she didn't know what was going to happen.

She'd been the one to say their marriage would be strictly business—no hanky-panky, no confusion over what they were doing. So there would be no sex to muck anything up, making her feel closer to him—or farther away, depending. Her feelings for him would be based on how they operated together, how they got along, worked together, took care of the twins together.

"Smells amazing!" she heard Noah call from the living room.

She gave the sauce a stir, not even guilty that it was from a jar. Hey, infants and working and making dinner? Sauce from a jar.

Five minutes later, she had everything stirred in a big blue ceramic bowl and brought it to the table. There was no dining room in the cabin, but the kitchen was eat-in and big enough for a round table for six by the window.

"Come and get it," she called out.

He appeared in the kitchen doorway, looking at her like he intended to do just that. His blue eyes were intense on her. This wasn't about appreciation for cooking or anticipation of eating. This was desire—for the chef.

"Now that I put it out there," he said, "I can't stop thinking about it."

"About what?" she whispered, a plate of garlic bread in her hand.

"Second chances. Everything I am is about second chances right now. I screwed up things the worst with you, Sara. I'd give anything to make everything right."

She put down the garlic bread. And rushed into his arms and wrapped her legs around him like she was Rachel McAdams and he was Ryan Gosling in *The Notebook*.

Not bad for seven and a half weeks postpartum, she thought, their mouths meeting, their bodies pressed so tightly against each other that she truly felt like they were one. They kissed so fervently that her legs couldn't retain their hold and they slid down. He pressed her against the counter, kissing her harder, hotter, his hands roaming into her hair, down her back, up her back under the light cotton tank top she'd changed into.

Just go with it, she told herself. *Go with what you feel, what you want. That is how you get your groove back. Stop overthinking and just feel.*

"Uh-oh," he said, putting her hands on his shoulders, his forehead against hers. "You said this was a no-go if we get married."

"My way of taking some control of things," she said. "I don't know what I'm doing, Noah. I just know that I wanted to kiss you."

"Me too," he whispered.

"But, but, but, I don't want to get emotionally caught up in you. That's not good for me. That's what I need to avoid. And yes, sex will absolutely push me into that." She threw up her hands, then grabbed the plate of garlic bread to have something sturdy between them. "What am I doing?"

This was nuts. A minute ago, she was feeling and going with it. Now she was overthinking again and letting that do the controlling.

Why was this so damned hard?

Because she was scared, she suddenly realized. That was it. Scared of losing herself again. And getting hurt again.

"Let's eat, okay?" she said, pushing past him to the table.

"I'll try not to look at you like I want to devour you again," he said. "That wasn't a fair move."

For a woman who hasn't had sex since she conceived? So true. At least she was pretty sure that night was the last time. Willem had been obsessed with her menstrual cycle and planning, and once he'd hit on the right window, he'd ignored her.

Anyway. It had been a long time since anyone had looked at her the way Noah had just then. Kissed her like that. Made her want so much more.

She sat down and heaped some pasta on her plate, then busied herself eating. The rich, creamy pink pasta and bacon and peas were every bit as delicious and comforting as she'd expected.

"Mmm, this is so good," he said, reminding her of sex again. She paused, her fork in midair, and watched him twirl a forkful into his gorgeous mouth. He took a drink of his bottled beer, then looked at her. "I'm going to take your lead from here on in. On whether we get married, whether we continue that kiss. No pressure from me, Sara."

"I appreciate that."

"Oh, and I should qualify that comment about the second chance. I mean just having you with me. My partner. My wife. Having you back." He glanced down, then cleared this throat. "But not in a romantic sense. Just like you said. We tried that, and we both know what happened. There's way too much at stake to mess anything up between us."

She stared at him. Was he backtracking or did he mean that? Was he truly worried that he'd drive her away again? She wasn't sure.

She cleared her throat and then just nodded.

Great, she thought, pushing her pasta around on her plate. She had no idea what she wanted, what she was doing. But what he'd said helped put things in a stalling pattern, which was exactly what she and they did need.

Feeling better, she took a bite of garlic bread. She really had to get herself assigned to another of the retreat seminars. Because she felt a part of her groove burning brightly back inside her—the red-blooded woman who'd thought that piece of her was gone.

Thanks to Noah just *looking* at her, she knew it wasn't.

After dinner, Sara had excused herself to her room and tried to read a book from the living room shelves on animal husbandry, but she couldn't concentrate. What she needed was a walk, some space from Noah where he wasn't upstairs or downstairs, so aware of his presence in the cabin, despite the closed door and a gleaming gold lock on it.

That kiss just loomed a little *too* large.

Wow.

Now she'd had a taste of what it was to be an actual sexual person again, and there was an incredibly sexy man in the vicinity who made her legs feel all rubbery.

She found Noah in the kitchen, drinking a cup of coffee and going through a stack of invoices, his laptop open in front of him.

"Can I help with anything?" she asked, standing in the doorway.

He looked up at her, and for a split second she saw so much in his eyes, in his expression, but then he flipped neutral. "Nope. Just reconciling some inventory."

"I thought I'd go for a walk," she said. "Get some air. You've got the twins?"

"Absolutely. Go ahead."

What a luxury. To be a single mother of infants and to be able to do anything on her own, let alone take a refreshing walk. That was thanks to Noah.

He glanced at his watch. "The retreat group's final lecture of the evening is scheduled to go on until nine thirty, so you might want to head away from the lodge if you're looking for time alone."

Hmm. It was 9:10 now. Maybe she would actually head straight for the lodge and make sure all was well, that the lodge fridge had enough bottled waters and that the fruit bowls weren't depleted. She could catch the last of Connie's talk from just outside the doorway.

She checked on the twins, then headed back to the kitchen. "The babies are fast asleep. Thanks for letting me get some air. I appreciate it."

"Anytime," he said. "I mean that."

He did. That wasn't in doubt.

As she turned to go, she could feel his eyes on her. The pull to turn back, to just walk up to him and hug him for so many different reasons, was almost too strong. She forced herself to the door.

The moment it closed behind her, she let out a breath. Up ahead on the path toward the lodge, she saw a slim figure with long wavy hair. A retreat participant? She couldn't tell in the dim lighting offered by the light posts that dotted the paths every now and then. But when the woman turned slightly toward the sound of an owl hooting in the distance, she could see a pregnant belly. That was definitely Daisy Dawson.

"Daisy!" she called out in as hushed a voice as she could muster.

Daisy turned around, and Sara could tell she was straining to see. "Sara?"

Sara jogged over. "Taking a walk, getting some

air, a breather. Noah's watching the babies. Well, they're sleeping, but he put himself on twins duty."

Daisy grinned. "How'd he become father of the year?" she asked, then her eyes widened and she touched Sara's arm. "I'm sorry. I keep putting my foot in my mouth about that. I know he's not Annabel's dad. Or Chance's, of course. And clearly, you two have worked something out. But I need to stop thinking of my brother as Annabel's dad."

"He still thinks of himself that way. Of both babies. Talk about taking responsibility," she added with a chuckle, trying to make Daisy less uncomfortable.

"So…how does that work, exactly?" Daisy asked. "I mean, you're playing house, but you're not a couple and he's not their father."

She'd always admired Daisy's forthrightness. Her brother shared that with her. "Can I swear you to secrecy? I only want your discretion because I'm not sure I should be sharing your brother's private business, you know?"

"Promise," Daisy said, holding up two fingers.

"He proposed to me. A marriage-in-name-only kind of thing. He'd get to be the twins' father. I get the security of a home on the guest ranch I was raised on. He even offered me half his share of the place, Daisy. That's how serious he is."

Daisy stopped on the path, the moonlight filtering through the treetops and capturing her amazed expression. "Wow. I mean, I'm not surprised to hear any of it. But wow."

"Wow is right."

Daisy stared at her. "And *you* said, I ask nosily?"

"I said yes, then basically said I don't know. I *don't* know. For all the reasons you can imagine. You know my history with Noah. And after what I went through in my marriage, I want to stand on my own two feet. No one is dying. I'm not desperate. I'm not trying to save anyone's life. It'll be hard, but I can do this on my own. I have this great job now. A place to live that makes me feel safe and comforted."

"I get it," Daisy said. "It's like you want to say yes for some reasons and no for other reasons, and no side is stronger than the other."

"Exactly. So what do I do?" Sara asked on another chuckle but immediately sobered.

"Sometimes my secret dream is that someone amazing will propose to me," Daisy said, a hand on her belly. She sighed and stared up toward the moon. "I was dating the father for three months. The condom broke, and then suddenly he was scarce. When I found out I was pregnant and told him, he said he was really sorry but he wasn't serious about me and he was only in Cheyenne temporarily, and then he just disappeared."

"Oh, Daisy, I'm so sorry."

"I don't know what's in my future. Well, except being a single mother."

"I'm here for you," Sara said. "Anything you need, I'm here."

Daisy pulled her into a hug. "Thank you. A lot." She stepped back, and they resumed walking. "Is it terrible that I'm finding reasons to listen in on Connie's talks? She's so good."

Sara smiled. "I know! I'm doing the same thing. In fact, that's why I'm headed toward the lodge. To check that the fridge is stocked with enough water bottles."

"Um, that was *my* plan," Daisy said with an evil grin. "There's only about fifteen minutes left, so I don't feel too guilty."

They linked arms and kept walking, the pretty white clapboard lodge with its steeply pitched roof and wraparound porch coming into view.

"Let's go check that water," Sara said.

"And the fruit bowls and granola bar bowl," Daisy added with a nod.

They headed inside and walked over to the kitchenette in the corner. A rectangular bar table separated the kitchen from the room, and they stepped behind it, both quietly "taking inventory." Sara made a note to add more apples to the bowl for the morning.

"So let's go over the most important step to getting your groove back," Connie was saying to the participants seated before her in a semicircle. "Figuring out what you *want*."

Sara glanced at Daisy, who was riveted by Connie. Daisy pulled a small notebook and pen from her back pocket and jotted something down. Sara could just make out that it said, *What do I want?*

"Maybe you want your husband to cook two nights a week," Connie went on. "Maybe you want a more satisfying job. Or a raise. One hour to yourself every night. Or your teenaged daughter to stop talking to you disrespectfully. Maybe you want more intimacy with your husband. Or a divorce. Or to stop arguing with your mother. Maybe you want a week's vacation at a beach. Or to see Italy. Maybe you want to read more. Become a mother. Or not. Maybe you want to learn to knit or take a German class or go skydiving. Whatever it is you want, identify it. If there's more than one immediate thing, write down the top three things you want, no matter how big or how small."

"Man, she's good," Daisy whispered, jotting down the assignment and then flipping her notebook closed and returning it to her pocket.

Sara nodded, her attention on Connie's words. *What is it that I want? Really want?*

I want to feel safe in the world.

The answer came faster than Sara thought. There it was, loud as it could be in every part of her. *Safety.*

"And the next step?" Connie went on. "Making a list of what steps you can take to get what you want. For example, let's say you want more intimacy with your husband, who watches the game, then a movie, and you've barely said two words since either of you got home. Maybe you suggest *going* to a movie, even if you have to see something you're not all that interested in. Maybe you suddenly give him a neck and shoulder massage. Maybe when you get out of the car in the Home Depot parking lot, you take his hand. You can start and see where it leads. Little things can lead to results."

Huh. *Steps to feeling safe in the world. What makes me feel safe? Feeling financially secure. Being able to take care of my children. So having a good job, which I now have. A nice home, which I now have, even if it's not the most traditional living situation.*

And somehow, out of nowhere, Noah Dawson makes me feel safe.

So, I'm doing exactly what I need to in order to get what I want.

"Tomorrow, we'll talk more about what to do when those steps don't feel feasible," Connie said. "But tonight, our homework is to think about what we want and if we feel comfortable, to start making those lists of steps we can take to achieve our goal or goals." She looked around at the participants with a warm smile. "It's been a great first day, full of wonderful new experiences. This time is your own. Perhaps for an evening walk or back to your cabins to rest up for tomorrow. The lodge's fridge is stocked with beverages and snacks that are free for the taking, so help yourselves."

"We're a bit low on fruit for the morning," Daisy said. "I'll go pop by the kitchen and replenish, then I'll head home. I want to start my homework right away."

Sara grinned. "See you tomorrow, Daize."

She watched Daisy leave, feeling buoyed for both of them—and thinking she should pay Connie for eavesdropping so much on just the first day. She smiled as two women approached to grab bananas and noticed Tabitha Corey heading out of the lodge. Instead of turning right for the cabins, Tabitha went straight on the path that led to the creek.

Go talk to her. If she doesn't want company, her body language or expression will let you know and you'll give her space.

Sara grabbed two waters and two small bags of pretzels and followed her, hoping she wasn't overstepping.

She saw Tabitha sitting on one of the large rocks that faced the creek, her knees pulled up to her chest, her arms wrapped around her legs. Almost like a self-hug.

"Hi, Tabitha," Sara said gently so as not to startle her.

Tabitha turned around, eyes wide, but she seemed to relax when she saw it was Sara.

"Water and pretzels?" Sara offered, holding them out.

"Sure," Tabitha said. "I wanted to stop and take something to drink and nibble on, but I didn't want to get caught up in chatting with the group. I'm feeling pretty talked out, and I've barely said ten words all day."

"I know what you mean."

Tabitha tilted her head. "I'm sorry about your husband. I would have attended the funeral, but I didn't hear a thing about it."

Sara opened her water. "Willem was very clear about not wanting a funeral. He instructed his lawyer to spread his ashes in the Bear Ridge River at sunset."

Tabitha raised an eyebrow and looked a bit surprised.

"Our marriage was pretty awful," she admitted, and it felt good to say it aloud to someone besides Noah. The truth was the truth.

Tabitha gasped. "I thought you had this perfect life!"

"Oh, I'd say it was quite the opposite. I'm working on creating the right life for me and my twins, though."

Tabitha looked confused again, as if she'd probably thought Sara had only one child, a baby son. But Sara didn't want to get into the details.

"I've been eavesdropping on Connie's talks," Sara admitted, popping a pretzel into her mouth. "I find her so inspiring and helpful and comforting. I only caught the last five minutes, but luckily it was a wrap-up and I applied the question to my own life. What do I really want? I was surprised to have an immediate answer."

"Me too," Tabitha said. "I mean, I know what I want. How to achieve it, another story."

Sara was so curious. But she couldn't just ask Tabitha what she wanted. It was personal, and if her old friend wanted to share, that would be one thing.

"From the outside, I probably look pretty blessed," Tabitha said. "Well, if you don't look too closely at me lately." She flipped up a hank of her frizzy hair.

"You're clearly engaged," Sara prompted, gesturing at the at least two-carat diamond ring sparkling in the moonlight. She'd seen Tabitha with the endodontist with his movie star–like blond hair and easy laugh at a fund-raising barbecue once. They looked like the perfect couple. But who knew better than Sara at how deceiving appearances were?

Tabitha stared at her ring. "I opened up to my mother about how I'm not sure I even love Philip, that I'm not sure I can go through with the engagement. Want to know what she said to me this morning before I left for the retreat?" she asked, looking up at Sara. "She said, 'All this finding yourself nonsense will find you alone and miserable. Your father and I will be very disappointed if you ruin your opportunity for a good life.'"

"By marrying your fiancé?"

Tabitha nodded. "He's the son of close friends of my parents. I've known him a long time. He checks a lot of the boxes."

"Which ones?" Sara asked, hoping she wasn't going too far.

"Well, for one, my parents are often disappointed in me for this or that, and I had their absolute approval for, I think, the first time in dating Philip and 'getting yourself proposed to,' as my mother put it. She actually told me she was proud of me for accomplishing that." She shook her head and turned away.

"So you *don't* actually love him?"

"He's all right. He's a good person. He's a mansplainer and we don't agree politically, and there's not a lot of chemistry in bed, if you know what I mean." She sighed. "He has a lot of good qualities, though. And I'm twenty-nine and single, as my mom points out often. She always says, 'I don't know who you think is out there that would be better than Philip. No one you meet will be perfect. Especially a guy you fall madly in love with. He'll be the *worst*.'"

Sara thought back to the Noah Dawson of two years ago. Even overbearing mothers had a point sometimes.

"Over the years I did get my heart broken a couple times by guys I fell hard for," Tabitha added. "So I know what she means. But still. Am I really supposed to settle like this? Marry the guy who seems right but really isn't?" She burst into tears and covered her face with her hands, her ring glinting on her finger.

"I'm so glad you came here, Tabitha," Sara said. "At the very least, you have a week away from your parents and Philip to really think. And to apply Connie's questions."

"What if my mother is right? What if it's guy after guy, one who wants me, one I don't want, never two of us in love, and I end up alone? I want a husband. I want children." Her voice broke. "I met a guy in the coffee shop the other day. A cowboy. He said he was a bull rider, hoping to win big in the rodeo. The way he talked about the rodeo and his love for

it, how his dad took him to rodeos every weekend
as a kid, he just stole my heart. He wasn't even nec-
essarily flirting with me. He was just talking, Sara.
He probably has a serious girlfriend, because he left,
no name, no number, no nothing. But he made me
realize that guy *is* out there. A guy who could rivet
me that way, you know?"

Sara nodded. "I know. I always felt that way about
Noah Dawson. That no one would ever compare. He
wasn't ready when we were actually a couple. But
he's ready now."

But was Noah actually ready now? He'd told her
he fully agreed their marriage should be strictly platonic. That meant he didn't really trust himself with
her or with their relationship."

Still, they were working toward something. "If
circumstances hadn't brought me back to him…"

Huh. She hadn't really thought of it like that until
just now. Circumstances had brought her back. That
was how life worked.

"So if you hadn't lost Willem," Tabitha said,
"you'd still be in your awful marriage when the man
of your dreams was waiting here the whole time."

Sara gasped. That was exactly it. She nodded,
vaguely, trying to take it in, digest it, process it.
Things with Noah weren't going to be a fairy tale,
but right now, Sara needed to think of the twins.

"That means the right guy for me might be out there too. I can settle and have my parents' approval. Or I can work toward finding the right man for me. Who knows, he might be in line in front of me in a coffee shop. Or leading the advanced riding lessons at the stables I love going to every chance I get."

Sara gave Tabitha's hand a squeeze. "Sounds like you're answering a lot of your questions."

Tabitha nodded. "I need to go do my homework. Write down what I want and how to achieve it. One of the problems has always been that I do want my parents' approval. I always have. If I give Philip back his ring, they'll be not only disappointed but furious. They won't understand."

"Well, maybe it'll help to write down the steps you could take to deal with that," Sara said. "If a harmonious relationship with your parents is very important to you, then write down some ways you could keep that while doing what *you* need to do to be happy. Your parents aren't living your life. *You* are."

"I keep telling myself that, hoping it'll sink in," she said. She stood up, and so did Sara. "I'm so glad you came to talk. This has been really helpful."

"For me too," she said.

They hugged and then headed back up the trail toward the lodge. Tabitha turned left for the cabins and Sara went right for the foreman's cabin.

Ping. A text. She took out her phone. It was from Noah. Even the connection by text gave her a line of goose bumps up the nape of her neck.

Just got a text from the Converse County Gazette. The review of the ranch is running tomorrow. I have a stomachache.

The review will be glowing, she texted back. The place is amazing and the guests love it. 5 stars.

He texted back a smiley emoji and a thumbs-up.

It struck her that you could only control so much. Noah had done the hard work and should be proud and pleased and expect that glowing review. But who knew if the reporter was a jerk or prickly or didn't like the color forest green or chili or the horse Noah had chosen for his mini trail ride.

All she knew was that she wanted to get back to the cabin—to be close to him. To think about what she'd said, what Tabitha had said. The man of her dreams waiting here for her this whole time… Maybe the timing was finally right, even if they were talking about a platonic marriage. And maybe she should grasp onto how she felt and not let go. Taking a leap of faith was hardly a way to feel safe in the world.

Except Noah *did* make her feel safe.

And the exact opposite.

Chapter Ten

B-rrrrring! B-rrring!

Noah opened an eye, then aimed it toward his alarm clock—6:14 a.m. His alarm would go off at six thirty, but someone was pressing the doorbell to his cabin like it was on fire.

Ping! Ping-ping!

Now someone was texting him. He grabbed his phone. It was Daisy.

Oh my God, oh my God, oh my God, his sister texted. Open up! Hurry!

He pulled on jeans and rushed out of his bedroom, meeting Sara in her bathrobe on the stairs. "Something's wrong," he said, panic edging his voice. "The ranch or Daisy's baby?"

Sara's eyes widened. "Oh God." She practically flew down the stairs and unlocked the door.

Daisy came in, clutching her phone.

"Is the baby okay? Should I call nine-one-one?" Noah asked.

Daisy stared at him as though he had two heads. "The baby is fine! The review is up!"

Noah felt himself relax for exactly one second, then all his muscles bunched up again, and his stomach flip-flopped.

"Did you read it?" he asked. "Positive or negative?"

Daisy shook her head. "I haven't read it. I just saw the headline and hurried over."

"How's the headline?" Sara asked.

"Very neutral," Daisy said. "'Dawson Family Guest Ranch has grand reopening in Bear Ridge'"

Noah sucked in a breath. "Okay, read it."

Daisy nodded. "'The once famed and popular Dawson Family Guest Ranch, which reopened Friday after years closed, is an absolute delight.'" She jumped up and down as much as a six-months-pregnant woman could. "An absolute delight!" she repeated.

Noah's legs almost gave out in pure relief. He dropped down on the second step.

"'From the immaculate grounds to the family-friendly vibe,'" Daisy continued, "'the guest ranch is a paradise tucked away toward the woods in Bear Ridge and offers riding and lessons, retreat space, a full-service cafeteria, a lodge, a petting zoo, and bountiful, well-marked trails, including several that lead to the creek. Fishing gear is available for free rental. The cabins, like the entire ranch, manage to be rustic and modern at the same time and contain everything a guest might need. The horses are gentle, and even the sheep look happy to be living at the Dawson Family Guest Ranch.'" Daisy did a little dance, turning completely around. "Even the sheep look happy!" she repeated. "Could this be any better?"

"Congratulations, Noah," Sara said. She gave him a quick hug—too quick.

Then his sister did. "I say we celebrate with decaf and bagels and cream cheese. I have such a craving. Please tell me you have veggie cream cheese."

"I actually bought some the other night," Sara said with a grin. "Sesame bagels or plain or everything?"

"Everything, of course," Daisy said.

They headed into the kitchen, Daisy going for the coffee maker, Sara for the bagels and Noah for the fridge to get the cream cheese. When everything was ready, they all sat down and toasted with their coffee mugs.

"To the Dawson Family Guest Ranch," Sara said.

"Hear, hear," Noah added with a clink.

Noah's phone lit up. Every one of his brothers either called or texted, and Cowboy Joe texted, as did several of the staff.

I did this—and I can be the husband and father of your children that you want, he sent silently to Sara. He slugged down a gulp of coffee. Where the hell did that come from all of a sudden? Well, maybe not so all of a sudden, since he'd been lobbying for the position for days. But earning Sara's yes meant everything to him.

What are you thinking? he wanted to ask her as she sipped her coffee and read the review for herself on Daisy's phone.

A yes from Sara and his life would be complete.

A cry came from the nursery, and Sara headed upstairs. He wanted to go with her, to take care of the twins together, to be true partners. In the platonic sense of the word. At first he'd been hoping they could be more than platonic, but then he'd realized that was asking for trouble. He'd messed up terribly once with Sara and couldn't risk that again.

"Everything okay, brother dear?" Daisy asked, peering at him over the rim of her coffee mug. "You suddenly look like a guy who didn't just get a rave review from a major newspaper."

"I proposed to Sara," he whispered. "I don't think she's going to say yes."

"Well, I have one piece of advice for you," she whispered back. "And you can thank Connie Freedman and her talks for that. Find out what she wants—what she really wants—and see if that's something you can provide. Maybe she's unsure."

He stared at his sister. What Sara wanted? Didn't he know? "She wants security. After everything she's been through? The rug pulled out from under her? Lies and deceit? Being left penniless? She wants security. I can provide that on every level."

"Okay, she wants security. But I said what she *really* wants. You're going to have to dig deeper under the umbrella term, Noah."

"Umbrella term? *What?*"

"Security. What does that actually mean for Sara? To Sara? Is it about money? She has a good job. A comfortable home? She has that now. So what is it she *really* wants?"

Oh God. He was bad at this. "If you know, please tell me. Right this second."

"I don't know. But if you want to marry Sara, you need to find out. And make sure you can give it to her. Or there's no point."

What did Sara really want? Women were kind

of mysterious. Everyone knew that. Was this some deep, dark puzzle or something simple?

Sara came down the stairs, eyes shining with love for the baby in her arms—Chance. "Annabel's still asleep."

As his sister doted on Chance and Sara made a bottle for him, Noah stared at his bagel, wondering what Sara wanted and if he'd ever find out.

Over the weekend and the following days of the Get Your Groove Back retreat, Sara continued her—now sanctioned—eavesdropping on Connie's talks and did her homework. She'd let Connie know the second morning how inspiring she found the talks, and the life coach invited her to listen in on all the lectures. Daisy joined her often, writing in her note-book, and Sara thought her friend seemed more at peace about the idea of being a single mother. Sara had tried to engage Tabitha a few times, but her old friend had told her she just needed to do some deep soul searching and take long walks and rides and do her homework. On the final day of the retreat, Sara thought Tabitha looked as conflicted as she had the first day.

"I don't think my friend Tabitha got her groove back," Sara said as they straightened chairs in the lodge. "I wish I had all the answers."

"Me too. Because you could tell me if I should trust Jacob."

"Jacob?" Sara repeated.

"The dad," Daisy said, patting her belly. "He showed up on my doorstep last night and said he felt guilty about just running away. He isn't sure what he wants, though."

There was a lot of that going around.

"What did he say?" Sara asked.

"He just kept saying he felt guilty and a man shouldn't shirk his responsibilities and that maybe we could just take it day by day. What the hell is that? I'm six months pregnant. This isn't a dress rehearsal." She sighed. "Or maybe it is. Maybe we should get to know each other through this stage, knowing the baby is coming in three short months. Maybe we'll really see who we are." Daisy always looked so sure of herself, and right now, she seemed anything but. "What do you think, Sara?"

"Sounds to me like you want to try," Sara said.

"I have to, right? I feel like even though he disappointed me once, he is the baby's father, and he is asking for a chance. If I don't at least try, I might regret that."

"Do you still have feelings for him?" Sara asked.

Daisy nodded. "There's something there. I tamped all that down over the past months. I don't know if it's him or the fact that he is my baby's father and it's more that than anything. I just don't know, and I hate being so out of tune with myself."

"I know what you mean," Sara said, giving Daisy's hand a squeeze.

"Here's a photo of Jacob." Daisy held up her phone. "The face helps, and it shouldn't."

Sara stared at the picture of an extremely cute blond surfer cowboy–looking guy with twinkling green eyes and a wide smile.

"I feel like I was getting my groove back, and now here he comes, throwing everything up in the air again. I feel so off balance."

Sara nodded. "Factoring someone else in when you need to keep yourself steady isn't easy. I know that for sure. Want to know what else I know for sure?"

"What?" Daisy asked.

"Our kids are going to be besties raised together," she said.

Daisy brightened. "Instant BFFs."

Sara nodded. They both drank their waters and settled back.

"Does that mean you're going to marry Noah?" Daisy asked.

Huh. Maybe it did. "I decided that when I wake up tomorrow, the retreat over, I'll know. At least, I think I'll know."

Things between her and Noah had been a little odd the past several days. They'd kept to their routine with the twins, which worked really well, but she constantly had the feeling he was trying to figure something out about her. The way he'd listen—hard—when she spoke, narrowing his eyes as if working to figure out some hidden meaning.

"Don't keep me in suspense," Daisy said. "Promise."

She and Daisy had gotten so close. Sara didn't know what she'd do without her friendship. "Pinkie swear," she said, wrapping her little finger around Daisy's.

Daisy's phone pinged. She took it from her pocket and frowned. "Uh-oh. It's a text from Connie Freedman. Tabitha Corey seems to be missing. She didn't show up for a scheduled activity and she's not in her cabin. Connie said she did a brief search on horseback in all the usual places Tabitha seemed to like to go but couldn't find her. Connie's worried about her state of mind since she skipped the talk and dinner last night too."

Sara bolted up. "I'll let Noah know right away. You stay here so you can be a ground support for Connie and the other participants. We'll find her."

Daisy nodded but looked worried.

Sara rushed off toward the foreman's cabin, texting Noah along the way.

* * *

Sara walked the creek bank again, Noah about ten feet away doing a sweep of the area from the path through the woods. Dylan and Bea, two of the ranch hands, were also searching the grounds since they'd come to know the nooks and crannies so well. She and Noah had checked and rechecked all the usual places Tabitha might be. She hadn't left the property, per the cameras by the gates on the road leading out of the ranch. The horse she'd been assigned, Nutmeg, was in her stall in the barn. All the bikes were accounted for too. Tabitha had gone off on foot.

Where are you, Tabitha? she wondered, scouring in between trees and down the edging of the creek toward the water, praying she'd find her old friend sitting curled up. Noah had said they'd give it only another half hour, because it was possible Tabitha might be injured and unable to call for help, and he'd bring in the big guns—his brother Axel, the search-and-rescue expert, and his yellow lab, Dude, an expert tracker. They'd find Tabitha in no time.

But Sara was 99 percent sure that Tabitha was safe and just hiding herself away because it was the final day of the retreat and she wasn't ready to go home, hadn't figured out what to do about her problems.

She scoured the creek bank, straining to see in

the sunny glare. Wait—was that movement? And a glint of something purple?

Sara slowly inched forward, craning her neck. Yes! That was a hand. And a sparkly purple sneaker. Tabitha wore sparkly purple sneakers.

She took out her phone and texted Noah. I think I see her! Yes, it's her! Give me a little time. I'll text you if she's hurt and needs help. Otherwise I think we should just talk a bit.

Okay, he texted back. I'll let Daisy and Connie know she's been found.

Sara pocketed her phone, then softly called out, "Tabitha?"

Tabitha didn't turn around.

"Can I sit beside you?" Sara asked.

"'Kay," came a teary voice.

Oh God. What had happened?

Sara approached where Tabitha was wedged between two big rocks, which now explained how they'd missed her on the first sweep. There was brush cover on both sides of the area she was sitting. Sara sat a good foot away, facing the same direction as Tabitha so the woman wouldn't feel stared at or crowded or pressured.

"Why do I have the feeling you came to a decision someone didn't like?" Sara asked gently.

Tabitha's eyes were teary. She lifted her head and

leaned it back against the rock. "I called Philip about an hour ago and told him I was very sorry but that I couldn't marry him. I was honest and told him I cared about him but felt pressured into the engagement by him and my parents but that it wasn't what I wanted."

"Oh wow. How'd he take it?"

"He was upset, but in the end he said he admired my courage and wished me well. And he hung up."

"So why are you so upset?" Sara asked. Then she realized Tabitha must have called her parents next and told them her news.

"I called my mom afterward. It was so hard to make that call. But I explained that I didn't love Philip and I hated to disappoint her but I had to do what feels right to me."

"Good for you!" Sara said—despite knowing full well her mother must have come down hard on her.

"I thought so. I felt so proud that I was standing up for myself and my future. And I believed, really believed, that I'd come first with my mom, you know? That she'd care more about me and how I feel than about appearances. Well, she didn't." She dropped her head onto her arms and sobbed.

"Oh, Tabitha, I'm so sorry." Sara scooted over closer beside Tabitha and put her arm around the woman's shoulders.

Tabitha glanced up with a tear-streaked face. "My mom said marriage wasn't about dumb lust and why did I think there was a 50 percent divorce rate. She said it was about partnership and well-matched couples building a future together."

Sara swallowed. Her own marriage to Noah would be a lot like the one Mrs. Corey described.

"But how can I sacrifice my happiness like that?" Tabitha asked. "It doesn't make any sense. It's sick, is what it is. But now my parents probably won't talk to me again."

Would Sara be sacrificing her happiness if she married Noah in this platonic arrangement? She would be happy feeling settled and secure. She would be happy living on the ranch. She would be happy that her twins would have a father, someone who loved them from the get-go.

But she wouldn't have a real marriage, the one she'd always dreamed of, the one Tabitha deserved, the one everyone deserved. Marriage with someone you loved and wanted to grow old with. Not a marriage that was first and foremost a business arrangement. Noah had her feeling so unsure about what he really felt, what he really wanted.

"I love my parents," Tabitha said. "I've never been able to handle when they're upset with me. And now they probably will disown me."

No way. That was nuts. Because she didn't want to marry the guy they thought she should? Because ending the engagement would cause a potential rift with their friends? "Do you really think so? They'll cut you out of the family?"

Tabitha could barely nod.

"Well, hell, Tabitha. That's not about love either. That's about control, and it's not fair. People who love and care about you and truly want the best for you don't cut you out of their life for not marrying the guy they think is right for you." Man, she was spitting mad. Sara felt like kicking something and shot up and did kick a small rock across the ground.

Tabitha hugged her knees to her chest. "I guess I'm really on my own now. In one fell swoop, I lost my fiancé and my parents of my own free will."

"The fiancé, yes. Your parents, no. I think you should write your mother an email, Sara. Right now. Speak directly and honestly to her, tell her exactly how you feel and why and how brokenhearted you are. You started on this path of honesty and being true to yourself. Continue on it. Your mother just might come around. And one parent is all you need to push the other."

Tabitha gave the smallest of shrugs. But Sara could see a glimmer of hope in her expression. "You think that might help?"

"I do."

Tabitha stood up, as well. "I'll go write it now." She glanced around at the woods. "I know I got a bunch of texts that I ignored—a few were my parents yelling at me, so I shut off my phone. I'm sure you guys and Connie were worried about where I was. I'm sorry."

"All that matters is that you're okay," Sara said.

Tabitha leaned over and hugged her. "Can we keep in touch after I leave tomorrow morning?"

"Of course!" Sara said. "And any time you need to get away or a place to go, you come straight to the ranch."

Tabitha gave a shaky smile. "Thanks. I just might."

They headed up the path to the lodge. Connie and Noah were waiting out front, and Connie came over.

"I'd love to talk a little if you're not too tired or done for the day," Tabitha said.

Connie squeezed Tabitha's hand. "How about over iced tea and really good cookies that I saved from dessert tonight?"

Tabitha smiled, then turned to Sara. "Thank you again. For everything. I'll see you in the morning to say goodbye?"

"Definitely."

She watched as Tabitha and Connie headed toward Connie's cabin, aware that Noah was walking over to where she stood by the directional sign.

"She okay?" he asked.

"She will be. She's on her way."

"Good," he said. "Ready to go home?"

Home. God, yes. How she loved the sound of that word and that it applied to here. The ranch. Dawson's. And the foreman's cabin.

She *was* home. But would she ever be truly settled?

It was pitch-dark when shrill cries woke Sara up. She glanced at her alarm—2:57 a.m. She couldn't tell which baby it was, but someone was making a racket—and these were higher-pitched cries than normal. Something was wrong.

Sara bolted out of bed and ran into the nursery to find Noah already there, lifting Chance out of his crib.

"He's really hot," Noah said, concern in his eyes. He laid a finger to the baby's forehead. "Very, very hot."

Sara put her own finger to Chance's forehead and gasped. She ran for the thermometer in the bureau as Noah laid Chance down on the changing pad. Chance's temperature read 103.2. "That's way too high. I'm calling the pediatrician." She rushed into her room to get her phone, grateful she had the doctor in her contacts. The service answered right away, despite the fact that it was almost three in the morning. She explained about Chance's high fever and raspy breathing, and the service said the doctor on call would return her call as soon as possible. It took just a few minutes.

She flew back into the nursery, where Noah was pacing, gently bouncing Chance in his arms, which didn't affect the crying. And it usually did. "The doctor said the temperature was high enough that we should bring Chance to the ER since the fever is combined with fast breathing." Sara's eyes welled. She stood there, taking deep breaths, barely able to think.

"I've got Chance," Noah said. "Call Daisy and ask her to hurry over for emergency babysitting. It's 3:00 a.m., but that's what sisters are for."

Sara's body unlocked; a mission she understood. She called Daisy, who assured her she'd be right over. A few minutes later, Daisy had arrived in her pajamas and flip-flops.

Sara and Noah rushed out with Chance in his carrier. For the twenty minutes it took to get to the clinic, Chance was shrieking, his face ruddy and sweaty. A half hour after that, he'd been diagnosed with a common respiratory virus that had flared out of control. He'd be absolutely fine.

Sara wasn't, though. This was the first time one

of the babies had gotten very sick. The panic she'd felt had taken over, and she'd appreciated the calm, cool and collected voice of Noah, giving instructions, knowing, somehow, what to do.

Feeling safe in this world meant a lot of different things. Having her person, someone she could always lean on, count on, trust, was paramount to her, more so than she'd ever realized.

That person was Noah.

She needed to be practical, not hold out for something she'd stopped believing in.

The answer to what she really wanted was summed up in how they'd operated tonight. They had been true partners.

"I've been doing a lot of thinking this week," she told him when they shut the door behind Daisy, who'd gone back to the main house. Chance was upstairs in his crib, sleeping comfortably now that he'd had medication to bring his fever down. Annabel would be staying in the bassinet in the living room for a couple days until Chance was more on the mend. "About what I really want. And what I want is for us to get married in the partnership you proposed."

That he liked what she said was evident in his expression. "We were a pretty good team tonight," he said, shutting off the hall lights and heading for the stairs.

She walked up beside him. "Exactly. We were. I panicked and you were calm, cool and collected. I needed help, and you were there. Daisy was there. I like having support. It's vital."

"It is. And you can always count on me. Always."

"I believe that. Let's go to the town hall once Chance is well enough. Probably even tomorrow."

At the landing, he took both her hands. "This is going to be the start of something great for both of us. Try to get some sleep."

"You too," she said, walking across the hall to her room. "Good night."

He held her gaze. "Good night."

Back in bed, she pulled the quilt to her chin. In just a couple days, she'd be married. Noah Dawson would be her husband. Her life would be completely different than it had been a week ago.

She was where she should be, making plans that would benefit everyone—her, Noah and the twins. Plus, Daisy would truly get to be Aunt Daisy instead of just an honorary aunt.

She smiled and closed her eyes, but sleep eluded her. Nerves about marrying a man she had so much history with?

So many what-ifs ran through her mind. She turned over and pulled the pillow over her head.

She was marrying Noah Dawson. For her sake. For his sake. For the twins' sake.

She was marrying Noah Dawson because she *loved* him. She flipped off the quilt and got out of bed. Before she could stop herself, she walked out of her room and down the hall, and knocked on his door.

"Come on in," he said.

Please mean that. In every sense.

She opened the door and closed it behind her, which made Noah sit up in bed and stare at her.

She walked over to the bed and sat beside him. Then kissed him. Then again. And again.

Don't stop this, she sent to him telepathically. *Because if I'm marrying you, I'm marrying you right. With everything I feel.*

"You're sure about this?" he asked, his blue eyes glinting with desire.

"Very," she said and kissed him again.

"And it's safe?" he asked. "Timewise?"

"It's safe," she assured him.

He peeled off her tank top, his hands all over her breasts. She watched him take in every inch of her bare torso and could feel him hardening underneath her. She took off his T-shirt and tossed it aside, and then he flipped her over and removed her yoga pants, leaving on her none-too-sexy pink-and-green granny panties with the little bow.

"I think those are incredibly hot," he whispered, hooking a finger at the waistband.

She swallowed, her insides feeling like liquid heat. "I think you're incredibly hot."

In moments, his sweats joined her pants on the floor. He lifted up over her, bracing himself on his elbows, staring down at her, kissing her, his hands in her hair, on her breasts, her shoulders, moving down her stomach…

She writhed underneath him, needing him so badly she couldn't take it. His kisses trailed up her neck, then his mouth caught hers so passionately she heard herself moan. She was kissing his collarbone and chest as he reached into the bedside table and pulled out a condom, making quick work of putting it on.

The moment he was inside her, all thought left her head and she only *felt*. *I love you, I love you, I love you* echoing in her head.

She hadn't forgotten how amazing Noah Dawson was in bed. He easily brought her to climax and then went wild to the point she was surprised the bed didn't collapse. The Wild West every night? That was more than all right with her.

And suddenly he was lying on top of her, kissing her neck, her cheek, breathing hard. "Oh, Sara. That was something."

"Yes, it was," she said. "And I guess this means our arrangement will now need some modifying."

She felt him freeze. *Crud.*

He turned onto his side. "What do you mean?"

"Well, we just had sex, Noah. And we're getting married tomorrow or the next day."

"I thought—" He clamped his lips together.

Oh hell. "You thought *what*?"

"I thought this was about tonight," he said hesitantly. "About the culmination of a rough night. Our marriage is supposed to be—" Again the lips clamped down.

"A platonic partnership," she finished for him, the ice in her voice surprising even her.

And clearly it surprised him, because his gaze swung to hers. "Sara, being platonic was your idea and a good one. A necessary one for me to make sure the marriage is a success. We need to be on the best path forward."

The best path forward? Good God. What self-help podcasts had he been listening to? Could he really want a platonic relationship at this point? Did he really not love her enough to make it work in all regards this time around?

Maybe he didn't.

"I think I hear Annabel," she said, grabbing her top and yoga pants and quickly putting them on. She darted out of the room and into the living room, where Annabel was sleeping in her bassinet for the time being.

She dropped down on the sofa beside the bassinet and looked out at the glow of moonlight amid the darkness. Noah had never veered on what he wanted; she had to remember that. He hadn't played games. He hadn't made sexual innuendos. He'd been crystal clear. Yeah, he'd brought up a second chance but then explained what he'd meant. A second chance to do things right by her. Not *with* her. He wasn't a man in love.

He wanted the twins and his former best friend to share his life on the ranch that he'd rebuilt.

She took a deep, steadying breath, feeling much calmer.

Well, at least she'd gotten great sex before entering into a sexless marriage. Tonight had been so damned good it would hold her for quite a while.

Or make her wish they could be together every night.

Partnership, partnership, partnership, she told herself. *Feeling safe in the world. Having someone you count on without all the craziness of lust and passion getting in the mix.*

A future to count on.

She heard footsteps coming down the stairs. "Sara? Can we talk?"

She stood, trying not to notice how incredibly sexy he looked. Trying to remember every moment of the past half hour. "I'm all right," she said. "Annabel's fine." She smiled and gestured to the bassinet. "Okay, that was an excuse to run away from you. But I'm fine."

"So…we're okay?" he asked. "*You're* okay?"

"I am," she assured him.

But she wasn't all that sure.

Chapter Eleven

The next morning, there was the expected awkward sidestepping as Sara and Noah ran into each other in the cabin a couple of times. Sara always had the mornings with the twins before Mrs. Pickles came so she could go to work, and Noah did his rounds on the ranch, but they'd been in the same place at the same time twice, both not quite looking at the other.

Last night, he'd accepted her "okay" and had followed her lead when she'd gone back to her room. The moment she'd heard his bedroom door close, she'd let out a huge sigh and then stared out the window at the night for what felt like hours. One moment—a half hour—they'd been so close, as close as two people could physically get. The next, separate bedrooms.

She'd felt really alone last night, but so aware of him down the hall, as always, and the dichotomy of that made her nuts. She had no idea how she'd managed to fall asleep, between thinking about their night together and what would happen in the morning: a trip to the town hall.

Now, they stood in front of the lodge at seven fifteen, preparing to say goodbye to their first guests. She forced her thoughts away from Noah as each of the participants shook their hands and let them know how much they'd enjoyed the ranch and what their favorite aspects had been. One guest, Zoe, admitted she'd cried saying goodbye to her horse, Lolly, with whom she'd felt a special bond, and she was already planning a future stay. Sara couldn't help but notice that Tabitha was looking particularly happy—and her engagement ring was no longer on her finger.

Her old friend pulled her aside for a hug. "So I did email my mom," Tabitha said. "I was very honest and emotional and put it all out there. That I couldn't marry a man I didn't love and didn't want to grow old with, but that I also couldn't bear to lose her and Dad's love over it, and if they were ready to disown me for disappointing them, I'd rethink the marriage."

Sara was surprised at that last part.

"I was bluffing," Tabitha admitted. "And seriously praying I knew my mom as well as I thought I did. I know my parents love me and I just had this feeling that if I really explained how I felt, my mother would come through."

"And she did?" Sara asked. From Tabitha's happy expression, that much was obvious.

Tabitha nodded. "With several hours to digest the news, my mother softened and said she realized what she was doing to me—the exact thing her own mother would have done to her. She said she was horrified when she realized that. She had a long talk with my dad, and they called me this morning and said I came first, it was my life, and they wanted me to be happy."

Sara was so relieved for Tabitha that she pulled her into another hug. "I'm so glad, Tabitha. Now you can go out there and find your true happiness."

"Exactly. Thank you for helping me see that and for giving me good advice. I'll never forget that."

"Aw, that's what friends are for. We'll keep in touch?"

Tabitha nodded, and they exchanged cell numbers, and then it was time for the group to board the van.

"What was that all about?" Noah asked as they waved at the van pulling away.

"Tabitha Corey got her groove back," Sara said. *By standing up for herself. By knowing what she truly wanted beyond the obvious and finding a way to make it happen. She broke her engagement and kept her parents in her life.* Sara was very impressed.

Noah grinned. "Good. The six new groups coming today aren't part of any retreats. We have two sets of couples, a few families, and friends looking for some nature time."

"They're all set to arrive at one o'clock?" she asked.

"Yup. We'll have a group orientation. After this, the orientations won't be in big groups—it just worked out that way since they were all arriving around the same time on the same day. Some of the guests will be staying a couple days, some four, some a week. Things are going to get a lot busier around here now that we'll have constantly arriving and departing guests. It's all thanks to the great review in the *Gazette*. We're booked, every cabin, every day, throughout midfall. I even have some bookings through winter at this point."

"That's great!" she said, wishing she could hug him. But she stayed put. "And Chance's temperature has been normal for over twelve hours, so I'm confident he's on the mend. We have a few solid hours to go get ourselves married before we'll need to be back and focus on the ranch."

Thank heavens for Daisy; she'd gone to the foreman's cabin about a half hour ago to babysit while Sara and Noah said goodbye to the guests, and she'd watch the twins until they returned from the town hall.

With gold rings on.

Noah was staring at her, clearly looking for hesitation, for upset, for a change of heart, but she had her neutrally pleasant face on. She wanted to do this. "Well, the staff knows what they need to do to get ready for the coming guests, so we can go anytime."

"I'd like to change, of course," she said. "I mean, I know it's not a big-deal wedding, but I don't want to get married in an employee shirt and denim shorts."

"Me either," he said with a nod.

They walked back to the cabin, both briefly chatted with Daisy, who was with the twins in the living room, and they went upstairs, disappearing into their separate rooms. They'd agreed to meet downstairs at eight.

It was just past seven thirty. A half hour to decide what to wear to marry Noah Dawson. She went for a pale yellow sundress that skimmed her body but was forgiving with its drape, and her bronze sandals. She left her hair loose, dusted on a little makeup, put a small dab of perfume behind her ears and that was it. Ready to get married.

A knock at the door made her jump. Didn't Noah

know he shouldn't see the bride-to-be before the ceremony? She rolled her eyes at herself. As if it was that kind of wedding.

But it wasn't Noah at the door, it was Daisy.

"Just checking if you need any help getting ready," Daisy said, sitting down on the edge of Sara's bed. "From the looks of you, you *are* ready. You look so pretty, Sara."

"Thank you for saying that, but it's not like it matters. *Pretty* and *romantic* aren't key words for these coming nuptials."

Daisy bit her lip and twisted her long hair up and let it drop over one shoulder. "Kind of reminds me of my own love life. Or lack thereof. Every time Jacob uses the phrase I *want to try*, I want to scream," she said. "I almost feel like the two of us are only getting back together for the sake of the baby. Not because there's anything between us anymore. But maybe that should be all that matters. The baby."

"I guess people end up together for lots of different reasons," Sara said. "What really matters is what *you* want, Daisy. What's right for you. I do believe that marrying Noah is right for *me*. Yeah—for the twins too, but for *me*. For a lot of reasons."

Daisy nodded thoughtfully. "And like I said, I'm just glad we finally get to be sisters." She stood up, a hand on her belly. "You've always felt like family, and now you will be. And I get to be Aunt Daisy for real."

Sara grinned and hugged her sister-in-law-to-be. "I don't know what I'd do without you."

Daisy grinned and glanced at her watch. "You'd better get downstairs, or you'll be late for your own wedding."

The town hall opened at eight thirty. Noah wanted to be among the first so they wouldn't have to wait around. She wasn't sure she would survive that.

Downstairs, she found Noah in a suit and his black Stetson. She hadn't expected him to dress up.

"You look very handsome," she said. She could barely take her eyes off him. Memories of last night hit her, and she forced the images of a completely *undressed* Noah Dawson out of her head. There would be no more of *that* in their lives.

"And you look absolutely beautiful," he said, the reverence in his voice catching her off guard. She could feel him staring at her, taking her in, liking what he saw.

But you prefer a lifetime of platonic partnership, she wanted to scream. *Safety over—*

Huh. She'd been so focused on how *she* needed to feel safe and secure that she hadn't really focused on why he was so dead set on a passionless marriage.

She knew that he needed the safety too. It wasn't

just about keeping Annabel and Chance in his life. It was about *her*. The thought hit Sara uneasily in the stomach, and she wasn't sure why. It wasn't as though she didn't know he was *avoiding* how he really felt or what was between them by insisting on a platonic marriage.

"Ready?" he asked.

Was she?

She found herself nodding, and they headed out, the brilliant sunshine and low seventies temperatures wasted on a quickie town hall ceremony that would last all of ten minutes. No reception. No wedding night.

Just…security. And maybe a couple of photos to commemorate the day. Taken by strangers, employees of the town hall who'd serve as witnesses.

She sighed as she got into his truck. She'd had the real wedding, complete with a princess ball gown, only white flowers—per Willem's decree—a jazz quartet and exceptional catering. Willem had hired a high-priced wedding planner and had apparently directed the woman not to let Sara make any changes to anything he'd already decided. Sara hadn't really cared. Back then, she was all about her father trying to fight prostate cancer, and that she'd danced with him at her wedding meant the world to her. The look on her father's face as he'd stood up with all the strength he could muster for that dance had been priceless.

Life was about choices, and Sara had made hers for reasons she would always stand by. She would do the same about today's wedding.

Fifteen minutes later, they arrived at the brick building in the center of Bear Ridge. Sara saw a few people she knew out and about, folks heading into the coffee shop, the diner, and waiting for the post office to open. Just people going about their lives while she was about to undertake something so big, so important. She was getting married and barely getting married at the same time.

Upstairs, they found the Weddings Performed Here sign on the second door on the right. Inside the large waiting area with benches and chairs and a lot of mirrors on the walls, another couple was already there, also clearly wanting to beat any possible rush at eight thirty on a random weekday. Sara imagined the couple was in a similar boat to her and Noah. An arrangement-type marriage. Needing to get it done before work. Even if the bride was in a strapless, above-the-knee white ball gown and white cowboy boots, and the groom was in a tux with a neon purple tie and black cowboy boots. Even if the bride held a beautiful bouquet of pink and red roses. Sara did not have a bouquet. Still, she liked to imagine the couple was getting married out of necessity instead of deep, abiding love. *Petty and small, Sara Mayhew,* she silently yelled at herself. *Don't wish a lack of love on anyone!*

She need not have worried. She watched the groom take the bride's face in his hands, staring deeply into her eyes, and say, "I'm the luckiest person on earth. To get to spend my life with you. I still can't believe it."

The bride leaned up on her toes to kiss her tall groom, wrapping her arms around his neck. "No, I'm the luckiest. I can't wait to become your wife."

Sara's shoulders slumped as pure envy socked her in the heart. She caught Noah eyeing the couple before turning away from them and fidgeting, pulling at his blue tie.

A door opened, and a middle-aged woman dressed in a powder blue suit with matching heels called the Hartley-Monkowski party. The couple made squealing sounds and hurried through the doorway after the woman, who closed it behind her.

"Guess we're next," Noah said, taking in a breath.

She nodded, biting the inside of her lower lip. A sheen of sweat broke out on the nape of her neck, despite the air-conditioning. Her sundress felt itchy. Her sandals suddenly felt too small. Her throat was dry and scratchy.

And standing next to her, looking like he might either faint or jump out the second-story window, was *her* groom-to-be. He seemed preoccupied, wasn't looking at her and did not remotely seem ready to do this.

To get married.

"Are you all right?" she asked him. *Please say no. Because this isn't feeling right.*

Why had it last night but not now?

"Just hitting me that we're actually getting married," he said. "Legally. Husband and wife. I'm about to become a married man." His expression was half wonder, half something else. Like fear.

"Strictly platonic partnership," she reminded him, peering at him closely.

"Platonic," he repeated. "But still it's legal. Official. We'll be married, and we'll both know it."

"Meaning?" she asked, staring at him. Where was he going with this?

"Meaning vows are serious stuff, Sara. We're about to vow to love, honor and cherish each other till death do us part."

And we're not going to mean it the way the first couple will, she thought. Sadly.

A small sob built deep in her throat. *Just remember why you're both here and doing this. Remember how you felt last night. Remember how scared and panicked you were. How grateful that you had Noah to count on.*

Partnership is a good thing. Not getting emotion and sex involved means things stay on an even keel. Always.

In other words, settling for certainty. Not that that word could ever be applied to anything in life. She thought about Tabitha, coming into her own, not settling for a life she didn't want. Sara might want the life Noah had offered—the husband, the family, the father for her kids, the ranch, the partnership, the team…but not the platonic part. How was she supposed to live as husband and wife with the man she loved—as essentially his *roommate*?

"Mayhew-Dawson party, we're ready for you," called a voice.

Sara glanced to the left; the woman in the powder blue suit stood in the doorway of the room where the ceremonies were performed. Beyond her, Sara could see the justice of the peace at the front of the room, standing in front of the windows.

She swallowed. Partnership. Safety in the world. Noah Dawson, her friend. The man she'd always loved.

And did love.

Oh God, she realized as she slowly turned toward the smiling woman in blue. She loved Noah too much for this.

Noah stood in front of the justice of the peace, a man he'd never met, let alone seen before, Sara beside him, looking like she might throw up. Her complexion was kind of pasty and green at the same time. Her expression at the trying-to-keep-it-together stage.

This was not how this was supposed to go. Butterflies were one thing. Nausea quite another.

He wanted this marriage. But not at the expense of Sara's happiness.

"Sara, if your heart isn't in this," he whispered, "let's just go home."

She frowned. Actually, she looked pissed as hell. "Just one moment," she said to the justice of the peace, then took Noah by the hand and led him toward the back of the room.

"My *heart* isn't supposed to be in this. It's not supposed to count at all, remember?" she muttered. She shook her head. "Tabitha almost married a man she didn't love to make her parents happy. Your sister is trying to figure out how she feels about her baby's father after he disappeared on her the past six months. I'm not sure doing the right thing should be this damned hard. And I'm not sure this is the right thing anymore. Do you want to know why, Noah? The beating-heart reason why?"

He had a feeling he was finally about to learn what it was that Sara really wanted.

"Yes," he said.

"Because I love you. Not like a friend. Not like a

partner I happen to be close to. I love you with everything I am, every part of me."

He sucked in a breath and stared at her. Of all the things she might have said, he hadn't been expecting *that*.

"I had to settle once before," she added. "And I paid dearly. I won't settle again. So unless you're in love with me too, I'd like to return to the ranch and spend my morning with my twins."

Something shuttered inside him—what thing exactly, he didn't know. A wall went up or a gate came crashing down.

He didn't want to talk about love. Or think about it. That wasn't what this marriage was supposed to be about. Teamwork and partnership and knowing where they stood and what they wanted from life and the future. A solid family.

"Sara, I—" He stopped talking, unsure what he wanted to say, what he felt.

"You know what, Noah? I don't think I'm flattering myself by saying that I think you do love me. And I mean love me in *all* the ways, every way, with every part of *you*. I think you always have, since we were teenagers. But you were scared then, and you're scared now."

He didn't like being told how he felt. At all. "Regardless," he said, that wall or gate making his voice sound so…cold. "We tried having a real relationship. Remember what happened? I drove you away."

"You're not that guy anymore. Everyone knows that. Especially me. And *you* know that."

Did he? He'd stepped up, yes. He'd changed his life. But wasn't he the same Noah Dawson he always was? Wasn't that guy who'd lost everything still inside him? Of course he was. Able to take over at any time.

"Then I guess we're going home," he said. "Wedding's off," he called to the justice of the peace and walked back through the door, two more couples in the waiting area now staring at them. Both women were looking at Sara as though she'd been cruelly left at the altar.

"She changed her mind," he snapped. "Not me." Oh God, now he was acting like a seven-year-old.

He glanced at Sara, whose cheeks were red. Oh hell. He'd screwed this up.

But he'd proposed something specific. She'd agreed. Then said no. Then said maybe. Then said yes. Then said no a few minutes ago.

Love, the kind she was talking about, the kind she wanted, was not supposed to be part of the arrangement.

And now you're going to drive her away again, he chastised himself as she stalked out the door and down the steps. She barged through the door into the parking lot. He wasn't even sure he'd find her waiting by his truck when he trailed after her.

He hurried downstairs and out the door. She was there, arms crossed over her chest, steam practically coming out of her ears.

"Sorry," he said. "Just got caught by surprise and let it get the better of me."

All that anger that had been on her face, in her body language? It turned to sadness. Defeat. "Same here, Noah. Same here."

What the hell was he going to do?

The new guests required all his attention, and he barely got to speak to Sara all afternoon. A few times they'd worked together, leading trail rides, supervising the petting zoo and going over the rules with the three sets of kids of varying ages, and pairing horses and riders. But they hadn't been in a position to talk. He'd have to wait until tonight.

And say what?

He was walking the path back toward the main barn when he saw his sister up toward the farmhouse with Jacob, her boyfriend, if he could be called that. The father of her baby. Noah had only met him a couple times, but something about the guy irked him. Jacob was polite, seemed okay enough, but there was just something that Noah couldn't put his finger on. And Daisy didn't look happy when he saw them together. He got the feeling his sister was forcing something she didn't feel.

Relationships didn't seem easy for *anyone*.

A few minutes later, he saw the boyfriend driving down the gravel road toward the gates. Daisy was heading toward him. She looked upset.

"Everything okay?" he asked her.

"You know it's not. This morning I expected to have a sister-in-law. Now I don't."

He almost smiled. "I know you love Sara, Daize. And I tried. But she wants more than I can give."

She stared at him. "You're lucky I'm not holding something. Because I'd bop you over the head with it. She wants more than you can give? Are you serious?"

He turned away, hardly interested in talking about this with his sister. "I've got a lot going on. At first, I just wanted to protect my interest in Annabel. Then her twin brother got ahold of me, and I started feeling like a father to them both. So I came up with an idea that would keep me and Sara in one place, give us both what we need."

"A roommate?" Sara asked, scrunching up her face.

"A *partner*," he corrected. "Without all the nonsense."

She snorted. "The nonsense of love? That nonsense?"

"How's Jacob?" he asked. Then regretted it. His sister was just calling him on what seemed ridiculous, and he could see how it might look that way to someone who wasn't him or Sara. They'd been through the wringer in different ways, and their needs were different. Daisy was six months pregnant and trying to make it work with her baby's father. He got that too. "Sorry," he said. "Been a long day. It's going to be a long night."

"Jacob is fine, by the way," she said. "We're trying. I don't know if it's working, but we're trying. The more time I spend with him, the less close I feel to him. How is that possible?"

"You probably just have no chemistry or much in common. Except for the baby," he added, eyeing her stomach. "I think it's great that you're both trying to make it work. But don't force something that isn't there."

"You are," Daisy said.

He stared at her, narrowing his eyes. "*I* am? How?"

"Trying to marry a woman you don't love," Daisy said. "So I'm not sure you should be giving advice on this subject."

"Who says I don't love Sara?" he asked, then froze. Of course he loved her. He knew that. But until he said the words out loud, he hadn't admitted it to himself. Or anyone else.

"Aha!" Daisy said, pointing at his chest. "I knew it. You are in love with Sara."

He scowled at her. "Doesn't matter. I'm not looking for romance. I just want a partnership marriage with certain parameters so nothing gets messed up. There's too much at stake."

"Mom once told me that no matter how bad things seemed at home between her and Dad, that marriage was a beautiful thing and I should know that I'd find my Mr. Right when I was ready and that marriage could be wonderful. I always felt bad because she didn't seem to really believe that—she just wanted to put it in my head, make up for what we were growing up with, seeing every day."

Their father had cheated on their mother a bunch of times. He and Daisy had both heard the arguments, the tears, the *I'm sorry, I'll never do it again.* Until the next time. And then his mother died, and his father was never quite the same. He still ran after women, but the loss had changed his father.

"I didn't need Mom and Dad's example to tell me relationships don't last. None of mine ever have. Including with Sara."

"You sabotaged that on purpose. Only you know why, Noah."

He rolled his eyes.

"Don't roll your eyes at me, Noah Dean Dawson.

You weren't ready then in any way, shape or form. You *got* ready and you changed your life. To the point that I came back when I swore I'd never live here again. You showed me what you can do, who you are, and I came home to be part of this. And because I was scared myself and needed a place to go where I could relax, where there was someone I could count on. You."

Oh hell. Now she was getting him all mushy. "Of course you can count on me, Daisy. I'd never let you down."

"I know you won't. And don't let *yourself* down. That's what you'll be doing if you let fear hold you back. You've got to be in it to get anything in this world. You know that."

"I'm doing that with the ranch. There's no way I'd blow the investment you all made in me. I've got enough riding on this place. I can't take more risks, Daisy. Not when it comes to Sara and the twins. I lose them, that's it."

"Well, Sara wants something very different, so you're going to lose her anyway. Kind of dopey of you not to *try*."

His phone pinged with a text. *Saved*, he thought. He pulled out the cell. His cowboy, Dylan. "Dylan needs me in the petting zoo. Runaway sheep."

"This conversation isn't over," Daisy said. "You and Sara both deserve better."

"Gotta run," he said and headed in the opposite direction.

Sisters, he thought. Good thing he had only one. His brothers liked to challenge him, but they didn't stand around talking about relationships the way Daisy did.

He headed over to the pasture beside the main barn, and between him and Dylan they got the runaway sheep back in his pen. He passed the petting zoo, stopping to watch his youngest guests, five-year-old Liam and his twin sister, Lyra, offer the little goats some pellets.

That'll be Annabel and Chance in just a few years, he thought, his heart close to bursting. He could just see them running around the ranch, playing with the farm animals, learning ranching by living here.

And because of you, they might not *be running around the ranch at all. In fact, they might be running around some other guy's ranch, someone else their father.*

If he couldn't give Sara what she wanted, she wasn't going to stay.

He couldn't live with that either.

Chapter Twelve

Sara wasn't sure why, but she couldn't stop thinking about Katherine Palmer. The midwife. She'd pushed the woman out of her head since the day after the bombshell in the lawyer's office, when Holton had assured her the midwife had retired, per calls he'd made to area hospitals and clinics and local OB practices she could be affiliated with and the Wyoming State Board of Nursing. Palmer's license had expired last month and she hadn't renewed it for the first time in thirty-seven years.

Holton had wanted to file a claim against Katherine Palmer, but until Sara had spoken to the woman herself, she didn't want him to do that. She knew what Willem had been capable of and could only guess what he'd threatened the midwife with. Once Sara had been assured the woman was retired and could never do anything remotely like what she'd done to Sara and Annabel again, she'd relaxed some and put Katherine Palmer out of her head until she was ready to confront her.

For some reason she couldn't put her finger on, the midwife had entered Sara's mind on the drive home from the town hall, along with the few lines Willem had written about her in his letter. She suddenly wanted to talk to Katherine, to understand why she'd done something so heinous. *How* she could have done it. No matter what Willem had threatened her with. A person who'd devoted her career to bringing new life into the world for almost forty years?

Sara sat on the couch in the foreman's cabin, the twins in their swings, staring at the sparkly mobiles hanging high above them, trying to figure out why it suddenly felt like time to pay the woman a visit. Maybe Sara was simply in fight mode. Maybe what had happened at the town hall, coming so close to marrying under terms she couldn't live by, had her ready to deal with everything that wasn't right.

She wasn't sure what talking to the woman would accomplish, but it had been hanging over her head since she'd learned the news back in the lawyer's office, and it felt like time to entirely put her past to rest.

When she heard Noah's key in the lock, she took a deep breath, preparing herself for anything. For him to say, *Actually, I don't love you, sorry.* Or, *Actually, I do, you're right, but sorry, I can't.* Either way, she lost. She'd confront the midwife, get that off her to-do list and figure out what she was going to do next. This new Sara Mayhew didn't leave things hanging. She might not exactly have her groove back, but she felt as if she was on her way.

"Crazy day," Noah said, coming into the living room. "Start, middle, finish and every moment in between. I wished I could have had just ten minutes to see you, talk to you."

"About what?" she asked. None too nicely.

"Just to check in, I guess."

"Thought so." Again, none too nicely. "I've made a decision," she said.

He paled, and she was struck by two things. One: that she knew him well enough to know he thought she was talking about leaving. And two: that it would truly tear him apart if she did leave.

But not enough to blast through the wall he'd erected where she was concerned. So that they could have a real relationship. Start a real future together.

He stood beside the coffee table, waiting. Looking…nervous.

"I'm going to see the midwife," she said. She expected him to relax since she wasn't talking about leaving at all, but he seemed more anxious, actually.

"Really? Why all of a sudden? Not that I don't think you should talk to her—I do. But just curious about why right now."

"Taking care of business," she said. "I need to close that chapter. And I need to hear why she did what she did. I need closure."

"I'm not sure she's the closure you're really after," he said.

She scowled. "Meaning? That I'm deflecting being upset about you? Yes, I'm upset about you. And us. But I'm done running away and seeking safety, Noah. Life is about risk. Being a parent is about risk. Love is about risk. I've avoided dealing with the midwife. But I'm going to face her."

He grimaced. "I'm coming with you whether you want me to or not."

"Good, because I do want you to," she said.

His entire body relaxed, and he sat down beside her, running a finger down each baby's cheek in their swings before turning his attention back to her. "And after you speak to her? Then what?"

"Then I move on mentally and emotionally from

what Willem attempted to do. I have my children—both of them. I close that part of my life so that I can start a new one. One in which I'm not scared or looking for anyone to take care of me."

"Sara, I—"

She was done with *Sara, I...* followed by either silence or Noah trying to explain himself. Unless he could say the words she needed to hear to marry him, any discussion of marriage was over.

"You know what?" she said, her eyes widening as something occurred to her. "I thought that feeling safe in the world was what I wanted and that I needed to give up other important values to have it for myself and the twins. But what I really want is to feel safe in the world at *my* own hands, Noah. Stand on my own two feet. I will never make another deal about my security, because I can support my children myself. It might not be easy, and as a single parent, my paycheck isn't going to stretch so far, but I've done the math, and I'll be fine if I'm careful. And I have been."

He stared at her, hard, and she knew his mind was churning, but she had no idea what he was thinking.

"You've always impressed the hell out of me," he said. "I understand. And I admire you."

That was all well and good. And if she were honest with herself, she'd admit he'd touched her deeply with that. But what she wanted, really wanted, was his *love*.

* * *

According to an online search, Katherine Palmer lived at 132-B Harris Road in Wellington, the town Sara had moved to when she'd accepted Willem's proposal. A quick map check showed Harris Road was near the center of town.

She decided to just show up, not call. If the woman wasn't home, Sara would simply wait until she turned up. It was kind of nutty, but the entire situation was insane, so there was no right way to go about it. Noah was unsettled about the whole thing but agreed that alerting Katherine that she wanted to talk to her might make the woman flee, and Sara would never get answers.

Because Wellington was an hour way, they'd decided to leave at eight this morning so they could be back by ten thirty or eleven at the latest, figuring they'd spend an hour or so with Katherine. Mrs. Pickles would babysit since Daisy needed to be on the job.

She was quiet on the way there, and she was grateful that Noah didn't try to fill the silence with conversation. He seemed to know she needed to just sit with her thoughts. She couldn't begin to explain how she felt at the moment anyway.

When Noah pulled up in front of an apartment complex, Sara could see 132 was the middle of three identical rows of garden apartments in a U shape around a green. In the driveway for apartment B, there was a small dumpster and a pod truck—as if someone was moving out.

"Maybe we got here just in time," Sara said. "Maybe she's moving." She sucked in a breath. "Let's knock."

They got out of his truck and headed to the front door. A small silver car was parked in front of the dumpster, so it looked like someone was home. Sara found herself unable to lift her arm to ring the bell. Her stomach churned, and she closed her eyes for a second. She squeezed Noah's hand, and he squeezed it back with an encouraging look at her. She was so damned grateful he was here, that he'd insisted on coming, because she wasn't sure if she would have asked him to otherwise, despite wanting him with her. Some things she could do alone. Some things she didn't want to. *This* was a didn't want to.

"Okay," she said under her breath and rang the bell.

She could hear footsteps. Sara's heart sped up. Katherine Palmer was about to open the door.

But the woman who appeared in the doorway was in her early thirties at most. The midwife was sixty-five years old. "Can I help you?" she asked.

Was this Katherine's daughter? she wondered. There was a definite resemblance. Similar auburn hair and hazel eyes, a similar fine-boned face.

"I'm looking for Katherine Palmer," Sara said. "My name is Sara. I was a patient of hers. Her last patient, actually."

"Oh," the woman said softly. "I'm sorry to tell you, but my mother passed away three days ago."

Sara turned to Noah, her throat closing up, her legs feeling like rubber. Of all the scenarios that had gone through her head the past several hours, this wasn't one of them.

"I'm sorry for your loss," Sara managed to say.

The woman gave a closemouthed smile of sorts. "You said your name is Sara. Sara *Perry*?"

Sara stared at her. "Why do you ask?" What did Palmer's daughter know? *Did* she know?

"My mom left a letter addressed to a Sara Perry," the woman explained. "I haven't had a chance to mail it or even drop it off. Between crying and trying to get the house sorted before the bank takes it…" She waved her hand by her face and then shook her head, her eyes welling. "Ignore me. Things are a mess."

She glanced at Noah. That the midwife had had financial problems wasn't a surprise. Willem had bribed her. She'd known that from the start.

"I am Sara Perry," she said. "And I am truly sorry for your loss. I lost my parents, and I know how painful it is."

The woman offered a small smile. "I'll just go

get the letter. It's on her bedside table. I think she wrote it the night before she passed. I was here the week prior, knowing how sick she was, and it wasn't there earlier."

"Was it cancer?" Sara asked.

The woman nodded. "The diagnosis came too late to do anything about it. I'll just go get the letter."

Katherine's daughter left the door ajar and walked up the stairs. Sara turned to Noah, unable to form words. He squeezed her hand.

"Another letter from beyond the grave," she finally said, shaking her head. "I don't know if I can bear it."

"Sounds like it might be a deathbed confession," he whispered.

She gnawed her lower lip. The woman returned, holding a letter, and she handed it to Sara.

"Thank you," Sara said. "And again, my condolences."

She nodded and closed the door.

Sara and Noah headed to his truck. She was done here, at least. She had a letter, which might explain things.

They got into Noah's pickup. "How about I drive a bit away from here, so you can read it in privacy. Without being right here, I mean."

"Actually, let's get out of this town entirely. Wellington is doubly ruined for me forever. Let's go back to Bear Ridge. You can park in town near the coffee shop—I'm going to need a boost of caffeine."

He nodded and started the truck, and once again she was so aware that he was right here when she needed someone who could see her through whatever the hell was in the letter. Explanation? Apology?

She held the letter in her hand as Noah drove the hour back to Bear Ridge. Finally, he parked near the coffee shop on Main Street.

"Ready?" he asked, gesturing at the letter.

"No. I wasn't ready for Willem's letter either. I almost wanted to flee the office before the lawyer could read it to me. Good thing I stayed."

Noah nodded. "I'll be right here. You can read it aloud or to yourself. Whichever you want."

"I'd rather read it aloud. So you hear what I hear." She cleared her throat and slit open the envelope. Inside were two pages, typed on white paper. It was signed with her full name—Katherine Marie Palmer—in black ink. She glanced at Noah, needing a gulp of him before she dived in. "Okay. Here goes."

Dear Sara,
Two weeks ago I was diagnosed with ovarian cancer, stage three. My doctors tell me it's inoperable. I did something terrible that I need

to rectify. I can't fix it, but I can tell you the truth. It's only two months later, and though that must feel like a long time to you, I feel better knowing it's not.

Your baby daughter didn't die at birth. Your husband, Willem Perry, told me he'd make up a devastating lie about my daughter and ruin her life if I didn't comply. He also bribed me by paying off tens of thousands of dollars of debt, which my late husband accumulated through gambling. Anyway, it's true that your daughter was born frail, but she was alive. He told me to back him up that she died during the birth. I was horrified but said I would for the reasons I stated. Then he muttered something about "Dawson." I don't know what that refers to, and as I left your home that evening, hoping to make it home before the big thunderstorm, he left too—with the baby in a car seat. I don't know where he took the newborn. But she was alive when she was born. Maybe the word Dawson will mean something to you? A start for finding your daughter?

This letter will be a shock. I don't know why your husband didn't want the girl. I only know that I can't go without making this as right as I can. By telling you the truth. May God for-

*give me. I won't ask your forgiveness, because
I don't deserve it. And I've taken enough from
you. I'm deeply ashamed. I don't know what
your husband would have done to my daughter had I refused, and because your daughter
did look so frail and small compared to her
brother, I rationalized that she would probably not make it. That was not my decision to
make. I hope I was wrong. I hope you find your
daughter healthy and get her back.*

Sincerely, Katherine Marie Palmer

Sara just stared at the words on the pages, unable to speak.

Noah took the letter and put it back in the envelope, then shoved it in his glove compartment. He
leaned over and took her in his arms, and she let
him, wrapping her own arms around him tightly as
she cried.

He didn't say a word; he just held her, which was
exactly what she needed.

Fifteen minutes later, she wiped under her eyes.
"I'm ready to go home," she said. "I have my closure.
And I never, ever want to think about her or Willem
or what they did or why again."

"Want to get some coffee first?" he asked, point-ing at the coffee shop two stores down.

"And a Boston cream doughnut," she said. "Maybe two."

He smiled and squeezed her hand. "Coming right up. Want to wait here or come in with me?"

"I'll wait here."

She watched him head in, her head clearing al-ready. By the time he came out with a white bag and two coffees in a tray, she was ready to put her past behind her.

She had no idea what the present would hold, though. Or where she and her twins would be in the near future.

Noah told Sara to take the day off. He'd matched her with a horse when she'd first agreed to take the assistant forewoman's job, and he was glad when she agreed that taking Bluebell for a ride in the acres of open pasture would be therapeutic after the heavy morning. The moment she'd ridden off, though, he missed her and wished he were beside her on Bolt. He didn't want her to be alone, even though he knew it was probably best for her right now.

He checked in with his staff, glad to hear every-thing was running smoothly. He was going to lead a trail ride for parents and kids who were new to horses, Dylan as his backup. As he met the group of six in the barn, three parents and three kids, he couldn't help but notice how the moms and dads doted on their children, listening to them, assuring them, being excited about the horses along with them. This was what he wanted for himself with Annabel and Chance, and because there was something fundamentally wrong with him deep inside, where he couldn't commit to Sara the way she needed, he was going to lose the twins.

With the kids on the gentlest of ponies and the adults on sweet quarter horses, they entered the small pasture and did a slow trot around the perimeter. There was hooting and laughing and big smiles from the entire group, and Noah gave easy instructions as he rode alongside the middle of the pack, Dylan at the rear.

And then out of nowhere, somehow, a little girl fell off her pony. Lyra Barnett, five years old.

Her face crumpled in tears under her helmet, and she just lay on the grass, not moving. Her father, a very fit man in his early forties named Mike Barnett, was beside her on the ground in a heartbeat, as were Noah and Dylan.

"I'll text our on-call doctor," Noah said, pulling out his phone.

The man held up a hand. "Hang on a second." He

turned his attention to his daughter. "Where does it hurt?"

The girl just cried.

"Daddy, is Lyra okay?" her twin brother asked, still on his pony.

Her father touched her leg, slowly inching his hands around both feet and the entirety of her legs. The girl didn't wince.

"I'm a doctor," Mike explained. "Nothing feels broken."

Noah's heart was beating like a hundred wild horses galloping. She was okay. Thank God.

Lyra cried harder, then wiped at her eyes. "I stink at riding horses."

"You were doing good until you fell off," her brother put in.

"I really was, right, Daddy?" Lyra asked, wiping under her eyes.

Her father smiled at her. "You sure were. Accidents happen, right?"

"Right," her brother said.

Lyra scowled at him. "Right," she said louder.

Mike Barnett smiled, and Noah had to also.

"Dylan, why don't you take the group into the next pasture," Noah said. "I'll have Sara join you." He quickly texted her.

Dylan nodded and helped Lyra's brother off his

pony so he could sit beside his family, and then he instructed the group to dismount, helping each kid off, and they all led the ponies and horses into the next pasture. He could see Sara already coming up the path in the golf cart, her expression grim.

"I'll run her over to the clinic in town," Mike said. "We're locals, so we're familiar with the place." He turned to his son. "I'll call Mommy and she'll take you to the creek to see if there are beavers and badgers and porcupines hanging around."

"The porcupines are my favorite," the little boy said.

Sara rushed over, concern in her eyes. Noah explained the situation, and she texted Daisy to pick up Mrs. Barnett from the lodge, where she was taking some R&R with a book and Cowboy Joe's lemonade and peach cobbler.

"Your wife will be here in two minutes," Sara assured him. She turned to the little girl. "Hi, Lyra. I'm Sara. Was this your first time on a pony?"

The girl shook her head. "My third time. I rode a pony at our birthday party."

Sara smiled. "I've been riding horses a long time. I fell off one time. I was thinking about something, and plop, right off on the ground. Luckily I wasn't hurt."

"I don't feel hurt anywhere," Lyra said. "I'm upset

that I'm not on Cupcake anymore." She looked at the sweet brown-and-white pony.

Her dad grinned and patted Lyra's back. "Well, let's have you checked out as a just-in-case, and if nothing is broken or sprained, we'll get you right back on Cupcake, okay?"

"'Kay, Daddy," she said.

Her mom arrived, and Daisy drove off in the golf cart with the family—father and daughter to their car by the gate, and then mother and son to the creek. Noah dropped back down to the ground, leaning his head against a fence post. "That was lucky. And close. If she'd gotten hurt…"

"Little kids get hurt. It's what happens. I like her dad's point of getting right back on the pony. That's the lesson, Noah."

"I don't need a lecture right now," he said, squinting up at her in the bright sunshine. "I feel bad enough as it is."

"I understand that," she said. "But you absolutely do need a lecture," she added, pushing her straw cowboy hat farther on her head and taking off down the path.

Every minute he pushed her farther and farther away, when all he wanted was to have her beside him.

Chapter Thirteen

As Noah finished his chores and rounds and got a welcome text from Mike Barnett that Lyra was absolutely fine, no broken bones or sprains or torn anything, he let out one hell of a breath. He knew that little kids got hurt. Of course he knew that. He'd broken at least five bones over his childhood from being too rough with himself and from incidents he had no control over, like tripping over a hole in the ground that his father hadn't taken care of. Kids got hurt. And yes, the important thing was to teach them to dust themselves off, if possible, and get back up.

He wasn't afraid of Annabel and Chance falling

off ponies; of course they would. Of course they'd have illnesses and mishaps. That was life.

So why the hell could he commit so fervently to them and not to Sara? Granted, he wasn't afraid of her getting hurt. He was paralyzed at the notion of giving in to the full range of his feelings for her. Once he did, he wouldn't be in control. That he understood, because he'd thought of little else the past two days. He had to remain in control of himself or he'd drive her off, one way or another. He couldn't ruin what they had—he wouldn't. And keeping things as professional as possible between them, as friendship based as possible, was the answer.

As he closed the main barn door, he saw Daisy coming toward him, on foot this time.

"So I have news," she said, stretching out her hand.

There was a ring on her finger. A small round diamond in a silver band.

"You're engaged?" he asked, his mouth dropping open.

"Jacob proposed this morning. He said he felt ready to ask me last night, but didn't have a ring, so went off to the jewelry shop to buy one." She looked at her hand.

"You don't look particularly happy," he said, then

regretted it. This wasn't his business. Or maybe it was. Of course it was. He was her brother.

"I feel good about it," she said, her eyes still on the ring.

"You feel good about it?" he repeated.

"Noah. I'm almost seven months pregnant. My baby's father proposed. We're going to make this work so that we can be a family. It's the right thing to do."

"Except you don't love Jacob. Does he love you?"

"He cares about me. He's committed to our family and our future, and he thinks we'll get there as time goes on and we share a life with our child."

He stared at her. "Get *where*? To love?"

"Yes, to love. We'll be raising a child together. Our goal will be the same. We'll be parents, committed to our baby. That alone will help us grow as a couple."

"God, Daisy. Is that how it's supposed to be?"

Now she stared at him. "Um, hello, pot talking trash about the kettle."

He scowled at her. "My situation is different. I'm protecting my stake in those twins. In not destroying my relationship with Sara."

"*Riiight*, little brother. With the woman you're madly in love with."

He froze, realizing how true that statement was. He was deeply in love with Sara.

"How can I not try?" Daisy asked, tears welling in her eyes. "Things might work out great with Jacob. He's my baby's father." She stared at him—hard. "I personally don't know how you *cannot* try, Noah."

With that, she walked off, leaving him so unsettled he had to sit back down against the barn.

Had a hay bale fallen on his head? That was how he felt. Absolutely gobsmacked.

And not sure where the hell to go from here.

To make this as easy on the two of them as possible, Sara was packed before she told Noah that she planned to move into the main house. She'd been thinking about doing just that ever since she'd left the town hall without a wedding ring on her finger. There'd been a lot going on and she'd pushed moving out of her head, but there was no way she could continue living in the cabin with Noah. Yes, he'd lose home access to the twins, but the way she saw it, that was his own damned fault.

Stubborn gets what stubborn deserves, she thought, instantly feeling bad for him. She didn't know exactly what it was going to take to get through to him, to blast through the concrete he'd built around his heart. She just knew she had to protect herself.

She had spoken to Daisy, swearing her to secrecy until she could talk to Noah about her decision, and

Daisy had offered her a bedroom in the farmhouse across from the nursery, which the twins would have. The downside was that the living arrangement was temporary. Daisy was newly engaged to her boyfriend, Jacob—boy, had Sara been surprised to hear the news—and Jacob would move in after the wedding. He was a businessman, something to do with imports and exports. She understood why Daisy wanted to marry him, despite, despite, despite.

Daisy and Jacob had talked about a July wedding, a couple weeks before her due date so that Daisy could have the wedding she wanted—a church ceremony and a big reception at the ranch with family and friends. If they were going to do this, she wanted to really do it.

Sara understood that more than anyone. And, at least it gave her a solid month in the farmhouse with her good friend until Daisy married and her husband moved in and Sara would move out, finding a place she could afford in town.

Now, Sara stood in the kitchen of the foreman's cabin, making a pot of coffee, knowing that Noah would be home in about ten minutes.

She was on her second cup of the bracing brew when she heard his key in the lock.

Her suitcases were beside the table. She'd thought about collecting the twins' baby stuff and putting it all near the door so that they could get into his truck quickly, but she knew what the sight of the swings and stroller and mats would do to him.

Her stomach churned. She hated hurting him. But he'd left her no choice but to do exactly what she was doing. She couldn't live this way with him, this quarter of a life.

"I smell coffee," he said with a smile as he appeared in the kitchen doorway. Then his gaze moved to the suitcases, and the smile disappeared. "You're leaving?"

"Moving up to the farmhouse. The twins will take the nursery that Daisy has already begun creating. The three of us will leave right before her wedding, when Jacob will move in."

He sighed and crossed his arms over his chest, quiet for a moment as he seemed to take in what she'd said. "I don't think she should be marrying him so fast. I get that they want to get married before the baby comes, but why not see how things go before committing like that?"

"Because they're committing," Sara pointed out.

He shrugged. "I guess they are." He stared at her suitcases. "I don't want you to go."

"Feel free to stop me, Noah." She tried a smile, but tears welled and she shoved her half-drunk coffee mug away.

"Sara, I..."

Oh God, not that.

Maybe the real problem with Noah Dawson was that he didn't love her. Maybe that was what he— and she—couldn't face.

But she'd bet everything she had that he *did* love her—very much. She knew it, she felt it, she believed. But until he could admit it to himself and open up the gates inside him, they were stuck.

"Will you help me load up the twins' stuff?" she asked. "I know it'll be hard for you, but I can't do it alone."

He grimaced. "Of course." He poured himself a cup of coffee, added cream and sugar, and took a couple long sips, then put the cup in the sink. "For what it's worth, I am sorry, Sara."

Tears stung her eyes. "Well, it's not worth all that much to me. I don't want you to be sorry. I want you to love me. I want us to raise Annabel and Chance together, be a family. I want us both to be happy. And if you really think you can be happy by shutting off half of yourself..."

He couldn't. But she was done talking, done arguing, done trying to convince him. It was time to go.

The expression on his face as he picked up one of the baby swings almost broke another piece of her heart.

But they silently loaded the pickup. Once back in the cabin, all that was left were the babies themselves in their carriers. She picked up one, then the other. Heavy, but she had this.

He stared at her, and then reached forward to take both carriers himself, but she walked out the door toward the truck before he could.

She could feel him just standing there and had no doubt his own heart was breaking. But by his own hand.

Noah had done double rounds on the ranch and finally made himself go home. Then he tried to stick to his bedroom, where he wouldn't be overly reminded of Sara or the twins. But he'd made love to Sara in this room. And every time he closed his eyes, he'd see them in bed. He'd never been so aware of how much he felt for her as he had that other night, when he'd stopped thinking so much and just let himself *feel*.

That he loved her like crazy wasn't in doubt.

He thought he heard a cry and bolted up and into the nursery, but the cribs, which were still there, were empty. Daisy had enough of a setup in the nursery she'd started making for her own child that they didn't need to move the cribs and dresser and glider right away.

He stood in the room, his gaze on the letters spelling out Annabel's and Chance's names on the cribs. He'd painted their names himself. He dropped down in the glider, where he'd sat so many nights, a baby in his arms, telling a story or just marveling at the precious infant he held. He thought about hearing Annabel's cries the night he'd found her. The note saying she was his.

The terror that had gripped him.

He'd been so damned scared of screwing up, but he hadn't. Hadn't screwed up at all in the seven weeks he'd taken care of Annabel.

And now he'd lost not only her but Chance, as well.

Instead of focusing on that, he kept going back to the previous thought. That he *hadn't* screwed up. Huh. Why the hell was he so focused on destroying his relationship with Sara when there was nothing to indicate he would—well, other than a history of doing just that? He had a history of failure, but he'd given himself an A-plus when it came to rebuilding the ranch and an A-plus in raising Annabel those first seven weeks.

He could handle a newborn baby as a bachelor rebuilding his family's legacy, but he couldn't handle his own feelings for the woman he loved with every fiber of his being?

He shot off the chair. Wanting to go get her. Get his woman. His life, his future, his everything. His Sara.

He sat back down. Once he'd allowed himself to really go there, there was no turning back. He'd be cracked wide-open. And his least favorite word in the English language: *vulnerable.*

He thought about the most vulnerable he'd ever felt. The day he'd read the letter his father had left him in his will. The whoppers in there. About how his dad believed he was the one to restore the Dawson Family Guest Ranch, that Bo Dawson hoped he would. *I believe in you*, his father had written. *I'm sorry I was such a failure. I know you can make things right, Noah. I know it. And knowing it gives me peace at going.*

Noah felt his eyes well. He took out the letter and read it for the fifth time, then put it back in the envelope and under his socks in the top drawer of his dresser. Even his father had owned up to his failures and looked to fresh starts—for Noah, at least, if not himself.

And Noah was going to sit in this empty, silent cabin when the woman he loved was a quarter mile up the road with the family he'd already made his own?

No, he wasn't. He opened his dresser drawer

again, reaching under the socks until he felt a small velvet box that had been there for two years now.

Sara sat outside on the porch of the farmhouse where she'd spent so much of her childhood, running between this house and the cabin. She loved this house as much as she did the foreman's cabin, and she was grateful to have a room here. She might not have what she really wanted in a getting-her-groove-back way, but at least she wasn't settling for what she didn't want. That was a no-go.

She and Daisy had had a long talk when she'd arrived with her stuff, after a grim-faced Noah had brought everything in, making a thousand trips up and down the stairs. Then he was gone, and she'd let herself burst into tears, Daisy comforting her. They'd talked for the past two hours, Daisy assuring her she was doing the right thing, Sara assuring Daisy she was too. Trying was paramount. Now Daisy was in her bedroom, working on her wedding plans for July. She'd asked Sara to be her maid of honor, and Sara had joyfully accepted. According to Daisy, they were still honorary aunts to each other's children, even if they weren't going to be sisters-in-law.

Daisy heard a truck coming up the road, then saw the headlights. Was that Noah?

She stood up as he parked. It *was* Noah.

If he was here to try to convince her to come back, he was wasting his breath. But damn, it was good to see him, and they'd only been apart for two hours.

He came around the side of the truck and walked up the porch steps. "I've been doing a lot of thinking."

Don't get your hopes up, she told herself. *He's going to suggest some kind of compromise.*

"You're absolutely right," he said, his blue eyes intense on her. "I'm letting fear control me. It's what did my father in, I understand that now. He failed, and then instead of picking himself up, he fell deeper into the hole."

She stared at him, her heart surging. Maybe she *could* hope a tiny bit.

"I've loved you so much for so long that you're a part of everything I am," he said. "I'm you and you're me and we're separate but the same. There's no me without you, Sara."

Tears welled in her eyes. She'd let herself hope a second ago, but he was taking her to the moon and the stars.

"I love you, Sara Mayhew. I'm in love with you. I want to spend my life with you and the twins. I want to be your husband in every sense of the word. I want to be Annabel and Chance's father. I love you. Even more than you could possibly want."

She grinned. "Is that possible?"

"Anything is possible now," he said, the moonlight shining down on him as he got on one knee, opening a little black velvet box. "Do me the honor of becoming my wife. Will you marry me?"

Sara gasped and barely managed to whisper, "Yes," before jumping into his arms and wrapping her arms around him. "I love you too."

He kissed her and she kissed him back, then he looked at her, and she could see the change in his eyes, in his expression. He slid the beautiful ring on her finger, then kissed her again. So passionately her legs buckled.

"Get a room!" called a voice from an upstairs window. "At the cabin so you don't wake the twins. I've got them till the morning. Go, lovebirds," Daisy added with a grin.

Noah laughed. "Thanks, Daisy. I owe you."

"Yeah, you do," his sister called back with a smile before poking her head back in.

"Let's go get that room," he said, taking Sara's hand.

And then they got in the truck and headed home, where they both belonged.

* * * * *

Don't miss Daisy's story, the next book in the
Dawson Family Ranch miniseries,

Wyoming Special Delivery

available April 2020 wherever Harlequin Special
Edition books and ebooks are sold!

And check out
Melissa Senate's Wyoming Multiples miniseries,

A Wyoming Christmas to Remember
A Promise for the Twins
To Keep Her Baby

Available now!

**WE HOPE YOU ENJOYED
THIS BOOK FROM**

**◆ HARLEQUIN
SPECIAL
EDITION**

Believe in love. Overcome obstacles. Find happiness.

Relate to finding comfort and strength in the
support of loved ones and enjoy the journey
no matter what life throws your way.

6 NEW BOOKS AVAILABLE EVERY MONTH!

#2749 A PROMISE TO KEEP
Return to the Double C • by Allison Leigh

When Jed Dalloway started over, ranching a mountain plot for his recluse boss saved him. So when hometown girl April Reed offers a deal to develop the land, to protect his ailing mentor, Jed tells her no sale. But his heart doesn't get the message...

#2750 THE MAYOR'S SECRET FORTUNE
The Fortunes of Texas: Rambling Rose • by Judy Duarte

When Steven Fortune proposes to Ellie Hernandez, the mayor of Rambling Rose, no one is more surprised than Ellie herself. Until recently, Steven was practically her enemy! But his offer of a marriage of convenience arrives at her weakest moment. Can they pull off a united front?

#2751 THE BEST INTENTIONS
Welcome to Starlight • by Michelle Major

A string of bad choices led Kaitlin Carmody to a fresh start in a small town. But Finn Samuelson, her boss's stubborn son, is certain she is taking advantage of his father and ruining his family's bank. When attraction interferes, Finn must decide if Kaitlin is really a threat to his family or its salvation.

#2752 THE MARRIAGE RESCUE
The Stone Gap Inn • by Shirley Jump

When a lost pup reunites Grady Jackson with his high school crush, he doesn't expect to become engaged! Marriage wasn't in dog groomer Beth Cooper's immediate plans, either. But if showing off her brand-new fiancé makes her dying father happy, how can she say, "I don't"?

#2753 A BABY AFFAIR
The Parent Portal • by Tara Taylor Quinn

Amelia Grace has gone through hell, but she's finally ready to be a mom—all by herself. Still, she never expected her sperm donor to appear, let alone spark an attraction like Dr. Craig Harmon does. But can Amelia make room for another person in her already growing family?

#2754 THE RIGHT MOMENT
Wildfire Ridge • by Heatherly Bell

After Joanne Brant is left at the altar, Hudson Decker must convince his best friend that Mr. Right is standing right in front of her! He missed his chance back in the day, but Hudson is sure now is the right moment for their second chance. Except Joanne's done giving people the chance to break her heart.

---

*When Jed Dalloway started over, ranching a
mountain plot for his recluse boss is what saved him.
So when hometown girl April Reed offers a deal
to develop the land, Jed tells her no sale.
But his heart doesn't get the message…*

*Read on for a sneak preview of
the next book in* New York Times *bestselling author
Allison Leigh's Return to the Double C miniseries,*
A Promise to Keep.

"Don't look at me like that, April."

She raised her gaze to his. "Like what?"

His fingers tightened in her hair and her mouth ran dry.
She swallowed. Moistened her lips.

She wasn't sure if she moved first. Or if it was him.

But then his mouth was on hers and like everything
else about him, she felt engulfed by an inferno. Or maybe
the burning was coming from inside her.

There was no way to know.

No reason to care.

Her hands slid up the granite chest, behind his neck,
where his skin felt even hotter beneath her fingertips, and
slipped through his thick hair, which was not hot, but
instead felt cool and unexpectedly silky.

His arm around her tightened, his hand pressing her
closer while his kiss deepened. Consuming. Exhilarating.

Her head was whirling, sounds roaring.

It was only a kiss.

But she was melting.

She was flying.

And then she realized the sounds weren't just inside her head.

Someone was laying on a horn.

She jerked back, her gaze skittering over Jed's as they both turned to peer through the curtain of white light shining over them.

"Mind getting at least one of these vehicles out of the way?" The shout was male and obviously amused.

"Oh for cryin'—" She exhaled. "That's my uncle Matthew," she told Jed, pushing him away. "And I'm sorry to say, but we are probably never going to live this down."

Don't miss
A Promise to Keep *by Allison Leigh,*
available March 2020 wherever
Harlequin Special Edition books and ebooks are sold.

Harlequin.com